I0452289

Close9 Publishing

The Meyer-Hoffman Affair

Ben Westerham was born in 1964 in London. After many years spent writing in bits and pieces, Ben now primarily writes crime, mystery and thriller fiction, often with a healthy serving of humour. He lives in rural Northamptonshire in the English Midlands.

The Meyer-Hoffman Affair

BEN WESTERHAM

Ben Westerham asserts the moral right to be
identified as the author of this work

Published by Close9 Publishing

ISBN: 978-1-911085-89-8

ALSO BY BEN WESTERHAM

ACKNOWLEDGMENTS

As always, my thanks go to my wonderful editor and my team of beta readers, whose input went a long way to improving the quality of the final book.

I'd also like to thank the town of Rye in Sussex, England for being such a beautiful little place and providing a wonderful setting for the larger part of this book. I hope I've gone some way to doing the town justice.

IT'S ALL ENGLISH TO ME

A word on the language that's used in this book, so you know what to expect. The version of English that is used here is British. This ought not to present much in the way of a problem for non-British readers. If you do find the occasional word or phrase a little odd, then I hope you still understand the essence of what is being said.

***

"A man's courage is like a horse that refuses a fence; you have got to take him by the head and cram him at it again. If you don't, he will funk worse next time. I hadn't enough courage to be able to take chances with it, though I was afraid of many things, the thing I feared most was being afraid."

John Buchan, Mr. Standfast.

* * *

CONTENTS

* * *

LONDON

The crowds on the broad, tree-lined promenade that was London's Victoria Embankment were substantial. Fleet-footed delivery boys and office messengers weaved their way around smartly dressed bankers and lawyers, on their way to or from important engagements, or newly-arrived tourists who wandered at their leisure, gawping at the sights shown in their guidebooks.

It was a fine spring day, the first such of 1913, but there remained something of a chill in the air and a stiff breeze blew in steadily off the dark, slowly moving waters of the Thames. After the long confines of an unpleasant winter, the populace at large were relieved to have the opportunity to escape their homes.

Whilst the crowds were a welcome harbinger of the changing year, they also presented something of a challenge to the nondescript gentleman with the light brown hair and rather large nose, whose task it was to follow the every move of a much taller figure up ahead. The taller man wore an especially fine top hat and twirled a long black cane as he made his way briskly through the crowds. Indeed, if not for that top hat, Alexander Templeman suspected he might well have lost his man by now, struggling, as he was, to simultaneously keep the fellow in sight and maintain sufficient distance so as not to draw attention to himself. The other man was, after all, Kurt von Luck, a suspected German agent.

The British Secret Intelligence Bureau had known for some months that their German counter-parts were obtaining copies of supposedly confidential Government papers, but neither the source of these papers nor the German agent involved had, as yet, been identified. The information being leaked concerned many facets of Government activity, including a draft of the recent annual budget and proposals for a review of local government boundaries.

However, by far the most concerning of these were papers from the War Office regarding the disposition of British Army units and Royal Navy ships, along with several papers from the Foreign Office discussing the Government's approach to diplomatic negotiations with a number of other European powers. It seemed only to be pure chance that, so far, none of these had presented a very serious threat to the safety of the nation, but the expectation was that such a situation could not continue for long. This extremely worrying matter had been made a priority for the Bureau, after details of these breaches began to filter back from British agents in Germany.

Templeman and fellow Bureau agent Henry Laidlaw had been assigned the task of establishing whether it was von Luck who was securing these papers and, if it was, who was passing them to him. Two other suspected German agents were being similarly kept under close observation by members of the Bureau. Thus far, no progress had been made in identifying either the source or the recipient.

Von Luck, a tall pale-faced man who walked with a distinct military gate, had been working at the German embassy, ostensibly as a senior diplomat, for the last fourteen months. For the most part, he engaged in all the usual activities of a diplomat, attending conferences and taking part in the ceaseless round of social engagements that occupied a considerable part of most diplomats time. However, during this period he had made several trips backs to his homeland, which provided ample opportunity for removing illicit documents from the country.

It was not so much his activities in London that cast the light of suspicion upon him; rather some portion of his previous record. In particular, he had been identified as one of those engaged in a disreputable attempt by a small group of Germans to blackmail three members of the French Ministry of the Interior into supplying confidential government information. The German ambassador in Paris had been able to persuade the French government that he was entirely blameless in the affair and those responsible had been sent home in disgrace, or so he claimed.

The similarities between the failed plot in Paris and that currently being investigated by the authorities in London was lost on no one. Both Templeman and Laiclaw remained exceedingly optimistic that their man was the mastermind behind the affair and they looked forward with much relish to unmasking him.

In the meantime, however, when it was his turn to follow von Luck during the morning, Templeman's time was occupied in a familiar pattern. He would wait for the German outside the opulent Blenheim Hotel opposite Hyde Park, then follow him down Park Lane to the German Embassy in Belgravia.

Most mornings at precisely eleven, a cab would draw up outside the embassy and carry the diplomat across town, always dropping him off at the same spot across the road from the Houses of Parliament. From there, he would make his way down on to the Embankment and spend the next hour walking alongside the Thames, then turning up to the Strand and on through Whitehall back to where he had started. What appeared to always be the same cab would be waiting to convey him either back to the Embassy or on to some pre-arranged engagement.

Templeman had wondered early on whether this choice of location for his morning exercise was merely because von Luck liked to stroll besides the river or if there might be some other motive. Perhaps beginning and ending his walk outside the Parliament buildings and strolling through the heartland of the British Government in Whitehall gave the diplomat some sort of daily encouragement to do his best, so that Germany might one day become as great a country.

On occasion, von Luck would stop alongside the river and spend a little while reading his newspaper. This particular morning was once such occasion. The diplomat purchased a newspaper from a vendor, then took a seat on an empty wooden bench that looked out across the Thames and there he began to peruse the day's news.

Templeman found another bench, from where he could observe the German while remaining out of his line of sight, and made a show of studying the barges and other shipping that made its way up and down the Thames. At times, the river traffic was so thick that it was difficult to see the water and it was a remarkable accomplishment, mused Templeman, that there were not a good many comings together.

As the minutes ticked by and the Englishman allowed himself to relax, he found his thoughts drifting to domestic matters and, in particular, his wife, Caroline, whom he had left at home preparing herself for a visit to her parents. The six months that had passed since their wedding day had been a gloriously happy time. Much to his surprise, he had adapted with ease to the new domestic routine set by Caroline, including the addition to their household of a part-time servant to help with the daily chores. The number of visitors to their little flat in Pimlico had grown extraordinarily, but even this he found he was able to take happily in his stride. This was all very different to his self-centred, easy going bachelor days, when he had no one other than himself to think of, free to come and go as he pleased and return home from his club as late as his fancy desired.

There had been discussions, at Caroline's prompting,

about the desirability of starting a family, but they had agreed they would first need to find a home more suitable in which to raise one. They had visions of a little house with a room for a nursery and a nanny, along with a garden in which the children could play and Caroline could grow her beloved dahlias. It was to be their own little piece of Paradise. Only the previous week, Caroline, with the aid of her mother, had begun the search for their new home; a rather tricky challenge given the relative paucity of the budget they had available to them.

The echoing chimes of Big Ben began to signal eleven o'clock and Templeman snapped out of his day dream with a start, for a moment concerned von Luck might have slipped away unnoticed. But, no, there he was, folding away his newspaper before checking his pocket watch, as if he was not content to accept the accuracy of the clock towering over the Houses of Parliament. Apparently satisfied that the hour mark had indeed been reached, he eased himself off the bench, pushed his newspaper into the hands of a passing boy, who looked somewhat bemused, then continued on his morning walk.

It was, considered Templeman, a disappointingly familiar routine that offered up no sign whatsoever that the German might possibly be involved in the securing of the leaked Government papers. He puffed out his cheeks, clambered back to his feet and took up his pursuit once more, glad that he would be handing on the baton to Henry Laidlaw once they returned to the German Embassy.

Von Luck's usual routine was to continue on to Waterloo Bridge, where he would then turn away from the river, up towards the Aldwych and the Strand, which he would then follow westwards, to Trafalgar Square and Whitehall. This morning, however, shortly after he had passed under Hungerford Bridge, the German turned into a small, narrow park that looked out on to the river. As he did so, his pace grew a little quicker.

Templeman felt his senses come alive at once. Finally,

something out of the ordinary. Perhaps all those hours and days spent forlornly tramping around after von Luck were about to have their reward. The Englishman turned on to the path into the park with his heart beating a little faster and his eyes fixed on his quarry.

It immediately became apparent to Templeman, however, that caution was the order of the day, since there were far fewer people for him to keep between himself and the German. He slowed his pace and dropped back a little. If some meaningful event did lay ahead, the last thing he wanted to do was to spook von Luck.

It crossed Templeman's mind that perhaps the German intended to meet an acquaintance in the gardens and his ideas of skulduggery were but wishful thinking. However, such a notion was promptly dispelled as the German strode on through the broad gateway that led out on to Villiers Street, sending a host of flapping, noisy pigeons to the wing as he did so.

Here, in the narrow street that ran alongside Charing Cross railway station, the crowds were once again thicker and Templeman began to regret having dropped back so far from von Luck. He quickened his step. It almost proved to be too late, for the German disappeared into a mass of bodies as he passed a tobacconists and, for a moment or two, Templeman thought he had lost his man.

But, just as the first sensations of panic began to grip the Englishman, he caught sight once more of von Luck, who was, unquestionably, now walking faster still. Was he, mused Templeman, doing nothing more than shortening his usual walk, perhaps necessitated by an appointment at the embassy? Or perhaps the German had some other business to attend to.

The shouts of a street trader seeking takers for his wooden toys echoed off the closely packed buildings as Templeman passed the man's barrow. Distracted by this performance, a well-to-do lady wearing the largest hat he was sure he'd seen so far that morning bumped into Templeman, whereupon she promptly turned to exchange apologies with him. It was a fateful moment, for, when the Englishman looked back up the street to see how much further progress his quarry had made, there was no sign of von Luck and this time he did not reappear from out of a crowd of bodies.

Templeman cursed his own carelessness, instantly certain this was the moment they had been waiting for, when von Luck would finally show his hand and the traitor leaking Government information would be unmasked. Templeman broke into a trot, weaving his way through the crowd. His body now tense and his heart rate quickening, he scanned every doorway and peered into every shadowy corner. Wherever there was a press of bodies, he lingered long enough to cast his gaze over every face. But as the opening on to the Strand loomed large ahead there remained no sign of the German.

A short distance before the Strand, Templeman spied a narrow road, barely more than an alleyway, leading off Villiers Street to his right. He stopped at the entrance to York Place and peered into the gloom, allowing his eyes a moment to adjust. There were no shop fronts here; rather, it appeared to be used primarily as some sort of storage or dumping area by the street vendors and shopkeepers. There were a number of carts on either side and small piles of wooden crates pressed up against walls. The smell of rotting vegetables and damp reached Templeman's nostrils as he stepped into the alleyway and the world fell oddly quiet, the hubbub of Villiers Street somehow unable to penetrate its narrow confines.

Templeman could not push away a peculiar sense of unease that grew upon him. It was as if his body was trying to warn him of an impending danger he could neither see nor hear. He steeled himself and pressed on, one careful step after another. There was a sudden movement at the far end of the short road and the Englishman turned his head at once, his body tensed, his eyes cutting sharply through the poor light. A tatty mongrel looked back at him, ran a thick tongue over its lips, then turned and walked out into the daylight.

The Englishman felt the tension in his body release at once and he shook his head, feeling foolish at his needless sense of fear. Aside from any other consideration, he had absolutely no certainty that von Luck had entered this road; indeed, at this very moment he could be strolling imperiously through Trafalgar Square. Once more Templeman cursed his own ineptitude. He clearly still had much to learn about his new trade as a secret service agent.

He was about to give up on exploring the unfamiliar and unwelcoming York Place when something caught his eye. He strained to see more clearly what it was, then took a couple of steps forward. Yes, there on the ground, poking out from behind a wheel of one of the carts, was a man's arm. A drunkard, sleeping off the worst of his night-time misdemeanours, thought Templeman, who took several steps forward.

"Good Lord," he exclaimed, the words leaving his lips before he could stop them.

He could now see all of the man, spread upon the hard, cold ground. It was clear he was no drunken vagrant. Far from it. The man wore a fine grey suit, his dark hair looked recently cut and his chin shaven. A bundle of bound papers lay on the ground in the lee of the cart. But most noticeable of all was the growing pool of blood that spilled from the man's torso.

Nausea welled up in Templeman's mouth and it took him a moment to regain control of himself before he could step right up to the body and drop down on to his haunches to see if the man might still be alive. As he reached out to take hold of the man's wrist, Templeman was aware of movement behind him. But something solid hit his head before he could turn to investigate and he slumped to the ground, unconscious.

THE RELUCTANT PATIENT

The sunlight that shone through the single window high in the whitewashed wall crept slowly across the exposed skin of the patient, who lay asleep in the narrow hospital bed. As it did so the man, whose head was wrapped tightly in a considerable length of new, white bandage, began to stir and murmur. If anyone else had been there to observe, they would have seen the man throw out an arm, as if in self-defence, and mutter incoherently. Then, with a snap, his eyes opened and he stared up at the ceiling in confusion.

There was a movement in the open doorway of the small single occupancy room, followed by the sound of a man's voice.

"Alex, you're back with us at last. Thought you were going to sleep right through to Christmas."

Alexander Templeman rolled his throbbing head carefully to one side, to find the smiling figure of Henry Laidlaw standing beside the bed. He opened his mouth to speak, but it was so dry the words failed to form correctly and the effort left his throat feeling sore.

"Steady on, old man. Let me get you a drink of water. And I'd best fetch the nurse as well. She's been waiting for you to come to, so she can check you over."

Henry Laidlaw returned several minutes later, followed into the room by a smartly uniformed nurse whose stern features and bustling demeanour spoke of one who tolerated no fuss. She gave Templeman a warm and welcome sensation of being in the hands of a true expert. After checking his temperature and heart rate, she eased him upright, so that he was sitting in the bed, seemingly propped up by several dozen pillows. Having furnished Templeman with a glass of pleasingly cool water, the nurse left Laidlaw with firm instructions not to over exert her patient, then departed.

"How are you feeling, old man?" asked Laidlaw. "Doctor said that was quite the blow you took to your head."

Templeman rubbed a hand tentatively over the mass of bandages.

"Sore," he replied. "But what happened to von Luck? And who was the dead man I stumbled upon?"

The slim, blonde-haired Laidlaw, with his seemingly ever-smiling face, pulled the sole chair across the room and sat down next to the bed. He was, in fact, four years older than Templeman, but looked as many years younger. And, although he was invariably given to seeing the world in a positive perspective his face now wore a serious look.

"Not the best of news about von Luck. He seems to have disappeared off the face of the Earth. We've had men out searching for him since we heard what had happened to you in York Place, but the man has either gone to ground, like the cunning old fox he is, or else he's on a ship crossing the Channel." Laidlaw shifted on the chair. "The man you found on the ground had been run through with a sword, or something similar. Chap was dead by the time the police reached the scene."

"Do you know who he was? Was it von Luck who did for him?" Templeman coughed, struggling to get his words out.

"Here, try a little more water." Laidlaw handed his colleague and friend the glass. When Templeman had satisfied his thirst and handed back the glass, Laidlaw continued. "The dead man was George Bettany. He worked at the Home Office. Middling rank. Access to a good deal of documentation. Hard to be certain, as things stand, but probably the source of the leaked documents, which would also confirm von Luck as being the German agent involved."

Templeman thought about what he had just been told before asking a further question. "But why would von Luck have wanted to kill him if he was such a good source of information?"

"Hard to say for certain. Could be von Luck was worried you were on to them, so acted to stop us from extracting information from Bettany. Or maybe the civil servant got too greedy. Started making excessive demands. Chaps like that can end up pushing their paymasters too far."

"I suppose you could be right about that," replied Templeman, his head dropping back against the pillows.

"Damn shame," observed Laidlaw. "I would have liked to see the Bureau have the chance to give Bettany a jolly good grilling. Who knows if there aren't more like him, lurking in the background."

Laidlaw stretched out and yawned. When he looked back at his friend, he appeared rather glum.

"Feeling tired, I suppose. To be expected after taking a blow to the head. I'm being inconsiderate keeping you awake."

"No, it's not that," replied Templeman, his words only just audible. There was a pause before he went on. "I don't think I'm up to the job of being a government agent. A spy. I can't see that I'm made of the right stuff."

Laidlaw sat up, his attention now sharply focused.

"Don't be so silly. I won't have a word of it. You've got all the brains and initiative a chap could possibly need for this business. Brave, too. And, be assured, you wouldn't have been offered the job in the first place if the Bureau wasn't entirely convinced you were up to it. Haven't seen them get it wrong even once yet."

"If I was half as good as you say, Bettany wouldn't be

lying in the morgue and von Luck half-way across the Channel. I was careless going into that alleyway and a child would have been less afraid than I was."

"Not a bit of it," asserted Laidlaw. "You've got pluck by the boatload. You showed that with the affair in Scotland last year and the little adventure you had in Vienna last month. I know men more experienced than you who wouldn't have been up to either of those challenges. You shouldn't think of selling yourself short, old chap."

"Pluck? Some might say foolhardiness," quipped Templeman, not sounding convinced by his friend's words.

The door to the little room swept open and the nurse bustled back into the room, followed by the many and varied sounds of a busy hospital.

"Visiting time is over now for you, Mr Laidlaw. Mr Templeman needs his rest and Mrs Templeman will be here shortly."

"Caroline," said Templeman. "Does she know what happened?" he asked his friend.

"She knows you've had a little bump on the head. Not been told about the other business though, if you get my drift. Didn't want to risk upsetting her. She's been with her parents all morning. Took us a while to track her down."

"Come along now, sir," insisted the nurse, looking over the top of her spectacles as Laidlaw rose to his feet.

"And remember," said the visitor to his friend, as he picked up his coat. "You did absolutely nothing wrong, so don't go blaming yourself one little bit for what happened."

"Thank you, Henry," replied the patient, a mere moment before a thermometer was pushed into his mouth and the nurse pulled her watch from a pocket in her uniform.

AN OPPORTUNITY EMERGES

Alexander Templeman sat alone and in silence in one of the comfortable, high-backed armchairs in the small, rather chilly office of Arthur Smallbone, private secretary to Sir Joshua Childers, head of the Secret Intelligence Bureau, or the Secret Service, as it was sometimes known. The occasional sound from the street two floors below drifted in through the partially open window.

Two days had passed since the incident in York Place and Templeman was fully recovered from the blow he had taken to the head. The two days had also been a time for reflection; an opportunity to weigh up the competing merits of his own views of his performance and the counter opinions of his good friend, Henry Laidlaw. He had also discussed the matter openly with his wife, Caroline, and had not held back from informing her of the death of George Bettany.

Caroline had, naturally, been greatly alarmed at the news of a murder and the thought that her beloved husband might have also been despatched. But, to her considerable credit, she had taken control of her emotions and the two of them had evaluated the situation with great care and deliberation. She tended towards the view held by Laidlaw, that her husband was a far better man than he gave himself credit for and that he could hardly be held responsible for the murder of Bettany. At the end, however, she agreed it must be for Templeman himself to make a decision on whether to continue working for the Bureau.

His conversation with Caroline passed once more through Templeman's mind as he waited to be summoned by Sir Joshua. Such violent danger had come so soon into their marriage and yet she was like a rock in the crashing, stormy seas; a safe place of shelter and support. Perhaps he might be letting her down if he was to give up this quickly. But the risks. His own inadequacies. Good Lord, why had he ever allowed himself to be talked into taking on the role? He shook his head and sighed.

But further deliberations were brought to an end as the door to Sir Joshua's room opened and Arthur Smallbone stepped out.

"Sir Joshua is ready to see you now, Templeman" he declared.

*

Sir Joshua Childers was a short, plump man with a chubby, welcoming face, much of which was covered by a large, bushy moustache that was somewhat out of fashion for the times. He was standing behind his vast oak desk, his podgy stomach jutting out in front of him.

As the door closed behind Templeman, Sir Joshua pulled the ever-present pipe from his mouth and waved it vaguely in the direction of an empty chair in front of his desk.

"Templeman. Splendid. Do take a seat," he instructed, in a deep, clear voice.

Templeman obeyed, though remained somewhat perched on the edge, while Sir Joshua pulled out his own chair and sat down behind the desk.

"Not sure if you've already met Vivian Eastwood," said the head of the Secret Intelligence Bureau. "He's our new chief of intelligence gathering. Poor old James Squire succumbed to the gout. Been afflicted with the damn condition for years, he has."

Templeman and Eastwood exchanged curt nods. They had, indeed, already met.

"Now then, Templeman, what's this I hear about you having second thoughts regards your suitability for this line of work? I've been telling Vivian what a splendid show you put up in Vienna last month. Saved our bacon there, you did. Not many would have been able to carry off a performance like that, hey, Vivian?"

"Absolutely not, Sir Joshua. This young man should be very proud of his performance, if you ask me."

Eastwood was a taller than average man with a long neck and a hawk-like nose that sat above a thick, largely grey moustache. When he spoke he did so with a rather high-pitched voice that seemed to Templeman to be at odds with his appearance.

"I feel I rather enjoyed more than my fair share of good fortune on that occasion, Sir Joshua. I seemed almost always to be one wrong turn from capture or facing certain death if my pursuers should choose only to take a little more care when shooting at me" replied Templeman, fiddling with his shirt collar.

"Nonsense, man. A little luck is always well earned. No one would have escaped such a tricky situation without displaying considerable skill and determination," insisted the senior man. "Saw that myself on service with Lord Roberts in Afghanistan and then again fighting the Boers. The best men always earn their own luck. It's not something that's freely given by the gods."

Templeman glanced down at the desk, then back up at Sir Joshua. "It didn't feel much like I was exercising any skill at the time, sir. I simply kept running, making my choices on the spur of the moment. It could so easily have gone very differently."

"I imagine you made a good many choices on the spur of the moment, Templeman," cut in Vivian Eastwood. "And yet here you now sit. It can't possibly have been mere luck that each time you made the correct choice. You may not have realised it at the time, and perhaps are struggling to appreciate it now, but it was down to your natural, inherent skill that you made the choices you did."

Templeman took a deep breath and straightened up in his chair.

"But George Bettany. If not for my clumsiness, the man would not now be dead," asserted Templeman.

"Nonsense," insisted Sit Joshua, leaning forward. "Von Luck had made up his mind to close down that operation in the most cynical way, regardless of your presence, and he would, no doubt, have taken the same barbarous course of action sooner or later. There would have been too much risk involved, from his point of view, to allow Bettany to live."

There was silence while Templeman, deep in thought, was observed closely by the other two men. Eventually, Templeman shook his head.

"I still think, Sir Joshua, that I'm not..."

"Alexander," cut in the head of the Bureau. "Before you consider making your decision final, please hear me out." Sir Joshua sat back in his chair and brought his hands up to rest on his stomach. "I consider myself a rather good judge of character. One of those things I happen to be very good at and I've made precious few wrong choices over the years, both here at the Bureau and before that during my days in the Army. I've developed a fine eye for what makes a man fit and proper for life in general and for this service in particular. Crass over confidence, arrogance if you like, are not what we need here. That tends a man towards making careless mistakes. A little modesty in a man and a willingness to ask himself if he could have done better is a welcome and rare trait. Add that to solid determination, a quick and accurate wit and a willingness to put King and country before yourself and you have the ideal agent for the Bureau. You fit the bill splendidly, Alexander, and I've never doubted it from the first."

Sir Joshua had never used his Christian name before and that he did so now left Templeman feeling hesitant and uncertain, touched by the warmth and personal nature of the appeal that had been made to him. He began to wonder if he could really be so sure of things, when those around him saw matters so very differently.

"That's quite the compliment," he replied, uncertainly. "I… I'm…"

"Why not give it one more go?" suggested Sir Joshua. "And if you feel no differently afterwards then I will, with reluctance, accept your resignation and wish you well." Sir Joshua picked up his pipe and inspected the bowl. "You might also like to consider the nature of the assignment I have for you," he added, a hint of conspiracy in his voice. "Since it seems likely to involve our good friend, Von Luck."

Templeman's eyes widened and he felt a surge of blood run through him.

"Von Luck? So soon?"

"It's as if the man is playing with us. Or perhaps he is himself an example of what I was referring to when I spoke of over confidence and arrogance," replied the head of the Bureau. "Regardless, he seems to be willing to present us with another opportunity to take him out of the game."

"Is he still in the country?" asked Templeman.

"I asked Vivian to join us because he has the very latest information on what we believe to be the intentions of our German counterparts and the most important operation of ours they are intent on undermining. Vivian, if you'd be so good."

"Thank you, Sir Joshua." Eastwood leaned forward, his forearms resting on the wooden arms of his chair. "We anticipate that some new, rather lethal weapons will be put to terrifying use in the forthcoming war, including the introduction of chemical warfare."

Templeman nodded. "I've read a little about that in the regular briefing papers."

"Quite so," continued Eastwood. "So you will have some

idea of the importance the Government and the military attaches to ensuring we are not left behind in the development of such weapons. Should we go to war bereft of these weapons, we could quickly find ourselves in a very tricky situation. It so happens that one of the leading German scientists in the field, Doctor Paul Meyer-Hoffman, is married to an English woman and very much sympathetic to this country, whilst also being appalled at the warmongering attitude of the Kaiser and his Chancellor, Von Bethmann Hollweg. Last month our Ambassador in Paris received a note smuggled to him by Meyer-Hoffman, pleading for help in escaping to this country."

"Extraordinary," exclaimed Templeman.

"Indeed and an opportunity not to be missed," said Eastwood.

"Am I to take it that Meyer-Hoffman cannot simply leave Germany behind and travel unhindered to this country?"

"That is correct," replied Eastwood. "Hence the secrecy involved with delivering the note to our French Ambassador. Meyer-Hoffman is correct to believe that he is under constant observation by the German police and their secret service, as we've seen for ourselves."

"Yes, that makes absolute sense," observed Templeman, eager to hear more.

"We soon enough put together a plan to bring Meyer-Hoffman out of Germany, but I'm afraid to say we were somewhat clumsy with our efforts and the attempt failed. Fortunately, we were able to somewhat retrieve the situation by making it appear as if it was a kidnapping attempt, rather than a willing effort on the part of Meyer-Hoffman. As far as we can ascertain, the German secret service believes that to be the case."

"And I assume from what's been said so far that we're going to try again?" asked Templeman, now so far towards the edge of the seat than any further movement would leave him on the floor.

"Indeed, we are and we would rather like you to be a part

of the effort."

There was no hesitation whatsoever in the reply. "Absolutely. I could hardly wish for a better opportunity to put recent matters right."

"Splendid," declared Sir Joshua. "Well, Vivian will bring you more fully up to speed. Everything is more or less ready to go now that we have you on board for the operation. It's a fine team that's been assembled and I only wish that I could have the opportunity to see the look on Von Luck's face when he realises what has happened."

"Yes, Sir Joshua," replied Templeman. "That would be a fine sight indeed."

A NEW ACCOMPLICE

As Alexander Templeman sat waiting, alone in a small and dimly lit office at the rear of the Bureau building, he contemplated the remarkable turnaround in his fortunes. There he had been, only twenty minutes earlier, on the very cusp of resigning his position with the Bureau, as a result of his uncertainties about his performance and suitability for the job. Then, not only had Sir Joshua made it very plain that he had the highest regard for him and was most keen he stay on, but within a mere two days of the murder of George Bettany an opportunity had arisen to hit back at the German agent involved.

He was keen as mustard now to press on with the new assignment and growing not a little impatient for the arrival of the man who would be running the operation to bring the German scientist, Meyer-Hoffman, safely to these shores. Templeman got to his feet and pulled out his pocket watch for the umpteenth time. Where in Heaven's name was Iain Moreland?

As if waiting in the wings for his prompt, the door to the room swept open and the tall, well-built figure of the Lowland Scot strode into the room.

"Sorry to keep you waiting, Alex. Been wrapped up with a

blessed request for information from Scotland Yard. Not one I could put off, I'm afraid." Moreland dropped a slim vanilla-coloured folder on the desk at the front of the room. "How are things? The old man persuaded you to sign up for my little caper, has he?" asked Moreland in what remained of his soft Lowland burr, as he ran the fingers of one hand through his short brown hair.

"He did, though he left the details to you."

"Mentioned Kurt von Luck, I suppose?" Moreland's keen brown eyes watched Templeman closely.

"He did, indeed. After what happened in York Place the other day he was well aware I'd be keen for a chance to make Von Luck pay for what he did."

Moreland nodded as he sat on a corner of the desk, one leg swinging backwards and forwards.

"Thought that would be the case. Never a pleasant thing to come upon a scene like that and such a callous act. He could simply have told George Bettany to continue on his way and re-arrange their clandestine meeting for some other time. But, you're fully recovered yourself? Doctors sorted out the concussion?"

"Yes, my head is fine now. Still have a slight bump, but no more pain."

"Excellent. You'd best take a seat, while I run you through the details." Moreland picked up the vanilla envelope and handed it to Templeman. "There's more information in there about Meyer-Hoffman, including his academic work and his wife. Did Sir Joshua mention she's English?"

"Vivian Eastwood mentioned it when he outlined things. Quite the good piece of fortune for us."

"Certainly is. Shouldn't imagine we'd have this chance otherwise. Well, I'll let you read that little lot later. For now, I'll outline our plan. It's got its risks, I'll admit, but with a fair wind I believe we can pull it off."

Templeman sat back, the envelope resting on his crossed legs, ready to take on board every detail of what he was about to be told. From the off, he wanted to make sure he gave this assignment his full and undivided attention.

"The problem, as we see things," commenced Moreland. "is that with the previous, failed attempt to get him out of Germany, Meyer-Hoffman is bound to be under even closer observation than he was to start with."

"Do you think the Germans will have bought the idea that it was a botched kidnapping?" asked Templeman.

"Possibly. Hopefully," replied Moreland. "But either way, it will have ensured they're on their toes from now on. He's far too important to them to go taking any chances. Quite frankly, I'm surprised they haven't locked him away in some castle high in the mountains, well out of harm's way. In matter of fact, they have given their approval for him to undertake a short tour of Europe, attending conferences in Geneva, Milan and Paris."

"I suppose he'll be accompanied, willingly or otherwise?"

"We're assuming there will be at least two German agents with him, possibly keeping themselves out of sight. It would make things a little easier for us if they were out in the open, but that's a minor matter. This forthcoming tour is simply too good an opportunity to miss, especially as it includes a visit to Paris, so our planning has focused on how best to make the most of it. The hardest part, we decided, will be throwing off the guards for long enough to put them effectively out of the game."

Templeman rubbed his head as he spoke again, "Wouldn't a little blow to the head allow us to tie them up and lock them in a hotel cupboard?"

Moreland smiled. "If it was on home soil, I don't doubt we'd take such an option. But we've been told to be considerate of the fact we'll be in France when we act. Sir Joshua is rather keen we don't upset the French. So, deception is to be the name of this game. We have a man lined up who has a passing resemblance to Meyer-Hoffman and we plan to switch one for the other in Paris. The stand-in will take a train to Brussels, closely followed by his guards, we hope, while the real Meyer-Hoffman will waste no time taking a train to Cherbourg, from where he will catch a ferry to Portsmouth."

"Cherbourg?" asked Templeman, a little confused. "Why send him all that way when he could instead make the shorter journey to Calais?"

"A good question. We are aware the Germans keep a watch on Calais. They did, for a time, do the same at Dover, until we began to close in on their man there, whereupon he fled across the Channel. It would be too big a risk to take, especially if our deception is unmasked sooner than we hope."

"Are we to meet him in Cherbourg?"

"No. That was another matter we debated at length, but decided our presence there might in itself increase the risk to Meyer-Hoffman. No, we'll meet him at Portsmouth, then accompany him on the train to London."

"So, everything depends on the switch going off well in Paris and the imposter not being unmasked in short order?"

"That's the long and the short of it, yes. It's not overly complicated and, all things considered, I think the odds of success are pretty good. That's often the case when an operation is kept simple."

"What about the chap standing in for Meyer-Hoffman? What will happen to him when the Germans realise they've been duped?"

"We intend to play a careful game there. Although he will be dressed very similarly to Meyer-Hoffman, he won't use the scientist's own clothes and when he checks into the hotel in Brussels, he will do so under his own name. That way he ought to be perfectly safe in claiming it's a simple case of mistaken identity."

"Hmm," mused Templeman, busy playing the whole thing through his mind. "Is he one of us, this stand-in?"

"No, he's a British-Belgium shoe-salesman who enjoys taking part in his local amateur dramatics society. He's been told just enough to know that he will be doing his country a good service. Of course, we've checked the fellow out from top to bottom and he's absolutely sound."

Templeman puffed out his cheeks and scratched at an ear. "And where does Von Luck come into all this?"

Moreland smiled. "He's the one responsible for keeping Meyer-Hoffman safely in German hands while he undertakes his tour. We have a source close to the German secret service who informed us about his role yesterday afternoon. Rather good timing, don't you think?"

Templeman came close to laughing. "Could hardly have been better timed, certainly from my perspective. I'll thoroughly enjoy my part in helping to destroy his reputation and in relieving the Germans of one of their key scientists."

"Good man. We've two more days until Meyer-Hoffman arrives in Geneva, then a further three until he reaches Paris, so there's plenty of time for you to get up to speed with the details, starting with that little folder."

Before Templeman could say anything more, there was a loud knock at the door.

"Yes," answered Moreland.

The door opened to reveal a man of similar age to Templeman, though with a shock of red hair and a face generously decorated with freckles.

"Sorry, sir. Need your signature for my travel warrant and if I don't set off right away I shall miss the ferry to Calais."

"That's alright, O'Malley. Have you two met before?" asked Moreland as he opened the desk drawer to retrieve pen and ink.

"No, I don't think we have, sir," answered the skinny new arrival.

"Alex, meet Daryl O'Malley. Daryl meet the infamous Alexander Templeman."

"Ah, you'll be the one who got himself a good adventure in Vienna last month."

"I did, indeed," responded Templeman. "Though referring to it as a good adventure is not quite the way I would describe it. Far too close a thing for comfort."

"Always jealous of an agent who gets an experience like that," smiled O'Malley. "Can't be doing with things being quiet. Bores me close to death itself."

"There we go," said Moreland, handing the signed slip back to the Irishman. "Paymaster given you sufficient funds?"

"Thank you, sir, and he has. Must have caught him on a good day," smiled O'Malley.

"Well, best of luck, though I don't imagine you'll be needing anything of the sort. See you back here in three days."

"Will do. Pleasure to meet you," added O'Malley, shaking hands with Templeman.

With that the Irishman departed, closing the door behind him.

"Quite the fellow," observed Templeman. "I imagine he's the life and soul of many a social engagement."

"I used to worry that might be a drawback for someone in our line of work, but, for O'Malley at least, it turns out precisely the opposite is true. His engaging character seems to ensure anyone and everyone he meets warms to him in an instant. Rather useful when it's proving difficult to get an agent close to a particular individual." Moreland put the pen and ink back in the drawer and closed it as he added, "He's got an assignment in Antwerp, via France. Ought not to be any difficulties, but you never can be certain about such things, especially with the times being as they are. The two of you should exchange notes when your assignments are all done with. I think you will learn a lot from the fellow."

"I shall look forward to the opportunity," replied Templeman.

THE WELCOME ARRIVAL

Iain Moreland and Alexander Templeman stood outside the
main building of Portsmouth Harbour railway station, at the
very end of the narrow jetty that arced out into the harbour
from the mainland. From behind them, on the other side of
the building, came the occasional hiss and fizz from the
railway engine that waited impatiently for the passengers
arriving on the morning ferry from Cherbourg. It would be
transporting many of them to London Waterloo station on
the ten minutes past ten departure and it was keen to leave
on time. It emphasised this by firing a burst of steam into the
air every so often, disturbing the noisy ranks of squabbling
seagulls that lined the roofs of the station buildings.

"Quite the smell," remarked Moreland as the wind blew
in another blast of sea air, laden with salt and the unpleasant
odour of seaweed that seemed to be hanging from every
exposed beam they could make out at water level.

"I'm not the best of sailors, I have to admit," came the
reply. "And the smell here is rather getting to me. Hard to
believe this is what they call a soft swell."

Moreland smiled. "I've been quite the traveller in the past
and, believe me, this is a mill pond compared to some of the
enormous seas I've experienced. God only knows how

anyone survives in the worst of weather."

"I didn't know you'd got around the place so much. Where have you been?" asked Templeman, turning to face his colleague. "Which parts of the world have you seen?"

"Quite a few, as it happens. Spent the best part of a year in North America, starting out with some relatives who live not far from New York. Vast country. Busy people, though not all terribly well educated. Then there was Constantinople. Peculiar place with some unusual customs, though quite a feast for the eyes. Persia was remarkable. So much history everywhere you go. A place I would be only too happy to return to. And then there was India. I've an elder brother who set up a tea plantation with partners in Ceylon and now lives there with his wife and two children. It's quite a long way from our childhood in the Scottish Lowlands."

"I'd say," remarked Templeman. "You make me rather jealous with all this travelling. I consider a trip across the English Channel here to be an adventure."

"Well it wasn't all a jolly time. Nearly got done for by a crocodile in Bengal. Saltwater type. Vicious beasts. A friend and I were studying a flock of birds on the far bank of a river when the crocodile starts drifting downstream towards us, not ten feet out into the water. Fortunately, the guide we were with spotted it and we ran back away from the water's edge just before the crocodile launched itself out of the water. Remarkably fast animal. Quite the scare it was, I can tell you. Must have been ten feet long, at least, that crocodile. Mind you, we were told they get a good deal bigger than that."

"Good Lord. Give up the birdwatching after that, did you?"

"We did. Who'd have thought birdwatching could be such a hazardous activity?" smiled Moreland.

A small tugboat came up the side of the jetty and began to steam past them, heading towards a pair of ships sitting a quarter of a mile or so out to sea.

"I'm rather partial to a good travel book," observed

Templeman. "Don't suppose you wrote up anything about your adventures?"

"I did, as it happens. Did most of my independent travelling after leaving the Army. But it costs a pretty penny, especially when you don't always have family member or friend to put you up, so I wrote articles for various newspapers and periodicals. Had a book published too. A short history of Ceylon."

"I'm impressed," replied Templeman "I'll have to track down a copy some time."

"There weren't all that many printed. Modest seller. So you might have a little trouble finding a copy. I'd lend you my own, except I haven't set eyes on it for at least a couple of years."

A porter crossed behind them, pushing an empty baggage trolley towards the arrivals area. It rattled and clattered loudly as its large steel-rimmed wheels rolled across the tar-stained oak decking.

"Lot of fellows at the Bureau seem to have served in the Army or Navy before joining up. Is it Sir Joshua's preference that men have forces experience?" asked Templeman.

"That's where they usually go fishing for new agents. Useful skills to be had there. You'll find there's more than one or two others, like me, with time spent working in military intelligence. Occasionally comes in handy knowing how to use a gun as well."

"Yes, I'd noticed that we seem to have a good number of men who've worked in military intelligence. When did you first get involved in that game?"

"Boer War. Arrived as a junior officer in the ranks after a few years' service. Vivian Eastwood spotted me. Saw something in me that he thought would make a good fit for his intelligence division and arranged for me to be transferred. I missed out on some rather hairy engagements as a result. Not altogether sure if that was a good thing or not."

"You knew Vivian Eastwood that far back? Was it him

who signed you up for the Bureau?"

"It was. I was one of the first few agents to be signed up when the Bureau opened for business. All very new back then and most of us didn't really know what we were doing. Very definitely had to make up a good deal as we went along, until Sir Joshua and Eastwood had got things properly set up. Must say, there's a little part of me that misses those madcap days."

A seagull dropped low in the air directly ahead of them, wavered erratically on the wind as it looked all around before letting out a piercing squawk and swept away low over the dark, churning sea.

"What got you into the Army? Family tradition?" asked Templeman.

"No. I sort of fell into it as a result of being unable to think of anything better to do. Originally thought I would follow my father into medicine, but changed my mind shortly before I was about to start my studies. The truth is, whilst it somewhat disappointed my father, I consider myself to have had a fortunate escape there. I doubt I would have lasted six months. Certainly not a year. To me that would have been a worse thing to do than coming clean before I was committed."

"Oh, absolutely," said Templeman, brushing his hair back into place, only for the wind to ruffle it again. "I think when a fellow knows something isn't right for him then it's his duty to speak up, even at the risk of upsetting others close to them."

For a time, the two men watched the little tug close on one of the two waiting ships and were amused when a seal briefly surfaced in the waters directly in front of them. If not for the distinct chill in the air, they might have been content to stay there half the day, watching the comings and goings of harbour life.

"Ah, that looks like her," said Moreland, eventually breaking the silence as he pointed towards a ferry steaming towards them between the land and the two waiting ships.

"At last," replied Templeman. "I suppose we'll only know if things have gone wrong if he's not on the boat?"

"We will. He was given strict instructions only to contact us once he'd left Paris if something had gone seriously wrong. Any contact runs the risk of the enemy making an interception."

"I understand Dr Meyer-Hoffman is an important figure in the German military set-up, but why is he so central to their efforts? Is there no one else who can pick up his work?"

"He's a chemist, by training, as you know. Studied physics and chemistry at university. A stand-out undergraduate, by all accounts. Once he'd graduated, he chose to continue his studies, now solely in chemistry, and eventually finished up with a teaching position at his alma mater. What got the attention of the Prussian military was his work developing gases to deal with pest infestations. One imagines from their point of view that enemy troops are just another form of pest."

"Not a pleasant thought," observed Templeman.

"Indeed not. But the Prussians made a good choice and Meyer-Hoffman has been central to their development of chemical weapons. In all likelihood, without his contribution they wouldn't be half as well advanced as they are. It got to the point where our own general staff had become rather worried, since our own progress in this area has only recently begun."

"So, it will be a win twice over for us if we can bring Meyer-Hoffman safely into the country. The Germans lose his services and we gain them."

"Precisely. And the very reason the Germans have been going to such lengths to keep him to themselves. As far as we can ascertain, they don't have anyone else as good as him."

"I'm surprised they let him out of the country at all if he's that important."

"Over confidence. They seem to think it impossible that anyone could spirit the doctor away from under their noses.

That and Meyer-Hoffman's insistence that he needs to attend conferences overseas in order to make progress with his research."

"And I suppose it was our good fortune that he chose to marry an English woman?"

"Indeed it was. I'm not sure we would have been able to persuade him to come here rather than France if not for her. They met in 1891 when the Meyer-Hoffman was on a trip to London. Like him, she was a little on the old side to still be unmarried. But she must have made quite the impact because they were married within the year. She went to live with him in Germany after that. We had to take care to ensure we had already brought her back to England before we did anything with the doctor. They're very much still in love with one another and he wouldn't countenance anything that put her at risk, even in a very minor way."

"Well, let's hope his contribution to our own development of chemical weapons at least brings us up to parity with the Germans before this damned war begins," commented Templeman.

"I'm rather hoping the people at the top come to some sort of understanding that avoids a war and all this turns out to be unnecessary," replied Moreland, though the tone of his voice betrayed the fact he had little hope this would, in fact, be the case.

"Indeed. That would the best possible outcome," said Templeman, as the ferry began to inch closer to the jetty.

"Come on, then," said Moreland. "Let's see if Meyer-Hoffman has made good his escape, or whether we are to return to London empty-handed."

NORTHWARD BOUND

The man they met from the ferry was a somewhat short, thin individual with little hair other than a greying monk's halo and a matching close cropped-beard and moustache. He looked more than a little flustered, doing his best to move quickly through the mass of bodies making their way towards the railway station, his gaze constantly scanning ahead of him. If he looked nervous, it was because he was.

Iain Moreland held up the photograph he had been given before leaving London and compared it with the face of the man they had quickly picked out from the crowd.

"That's the chap," he confirmed. "Very nearly a perfect likeness, apart from this photograph having been taken two years ago."

As the doctor cleared the customs post, carrying a modest leather suitcase and a small briefcase, Moreland and Templeman stepped forward to greet him.

"Dr Meyer-Hoffman?"

The German scientist hesitated, looking sharply from one man to the other.

"I'm Iain Moreland and this is Alexander Templeman. We're from the London office, here to welcome you back to England," smiled Moreland in the hope his own relaxed demeanour would help to put the scientist at ease.

"Ah, that is good. Very good," replied Meyer-Hoffman, the relief clear in his voice.

"Is that all your luggage?" asked Moreland.

"It is. Better I do not carry much. It would only slow me down."

"Very true. Well, let's not linger," said Moreland. "The Waterloo train leaves shortly and it would be best to board it promptly. Here, let me take your suitcase," offered Moreland.

The Bureau had reserved a compartment on the train entirely for the three of them, keen to take whatever precautions they could to ensure the scientist's safety. The three men found it without issue and closed themselves inside to await the train's departure.

"Pleasant crossing?" asked Templeman as Moreland slipped the scientist's suitcase on to the overhead baggage rack.

"Pleasant is not the right word," replied Meyer-Hoffman, in a soft, precise voice, his excellent English flecked through with a still noticeable German accent. "A member of the crew informed me it was a fine crossing, as good as could be expected. But I am not a man of the seas and even such weather as we have today was enough to bring me close to the sea sickness."

"Ah ha," remarked Moreland taking a seat next to the German. "It sounds rather like you have something in common with Alex, who also dislikes travelling the ocean waves."

"I feel certain man was made for travelling only on the land," said Meyer-Hoffman. "That says strange things about you English that you have made an empire of the seas. Perhaps your Viking blood provides you with some immunity to sea travel."

There was a murmur of amusement from the other two men and all three settled down, ready for the journey north to London. As they did so, Templeman studied the new arrival with a good deal of curiosity, observing the way he straightened his trouser legs so precisely and re-arranged the cuffs of his shirt and suit jacket with considerable care. It was clear the man also kept his moustache and beard neatly cropped and his fingernails well clipped, while his movements matched such fastidiousness, being both precise and economical.

"I'm afraid we'll be steering clear of the dining car," Moreland informed the doctor. "We're not expecting any trouble from here on in but it's best we keep you away from prying eyes as much as we can. The journey takes little more than an hour, then we can check you into your hotel and leave you free to enjoy a spot of lunch."

"My stomach would not enjoy any food for now," replied Meyer-Hoffman. "So the lack of it is no bad thing."

The sound of a sharp whistle from further along the platform pierced the air.

"Seems as though we're about ready to depart," observed Moreland, watching a short, rotund man labouring under the weight and bulk of two enormous suitcases struggling across the last few yards to the train.

As the man disappeared inside the train, slamming the door shut behind him, there was another loud blast on the whistle before the carriage lurched forward a little, stopped, then lurched onwards again. Smoke swirled all around them; in some places thin, twirling fingers that disappeared in a moment, in others solid impenetrable blocks that engulfed anything they encountered. And then they were easing out of the station, accompanied by the sharp, squealing sounds the wheels made on the rails.

As they cleared the jetty and left behind the sea, to be swallowed up by a mishmash of warehouses and other buildings, Moreland turned back to Meyer-Hoffman.

"So, no signs of any pursuit when you left Paris, as far as you could tell, doctor?"

"No, none," replied the German. "But you must understand, I am not equipped with the skills you possess. It may be I was followed, but, if so, no one attempted to stop me."

"I would imagine if Von Luck did have someone following you they would have intervened to stop you from boarding the ferry. More likely our ruse worked and they're still busy following your double to Brussels."

"A most ingenious idea," remarked Meyer-Hoffman. "But will the man not be punished when they discover what has happened?"

"No, we've arranged things so that he can plausibly pass as being entirely innocent of any involvement in our little deception. From what I hear, the chap was rather looking forward to it."

As the train started to pick up speed, they began to pass narrow roads lined with regimental rows of mid-Victorian red brick houses.

"My wife, Helen, she is safe and comfortable?" enquired the German.

"Indeed, she is," replied Moreland. "She's been staying with her sister in Bromley since she arrived back in England last week. Once we have settled you into your hotel, we'll arrange for your wife to travel up to London to join you."

"Good. Good. Helen, she is everything to me. Such a wife as no man could imagine is possible. Heaven must have looked down on me with kindness on the day we met."

"I know that feeling myself," said Templeman, who was about to add more when there was a sharp rap on the door to the compartment, followed by the appearance of the ticket inspector.

"Sorry to disturb you, gentlemen," said the ticket inspector. "But I have a message I'm told is most urgent. Would one of you be Mr Iain Moreland?"

"That's me," replied the older of the two agents.

"Here we are then, sir. Telegram was given to me just before the train left the station."

"Thank you," replied Moreland, taking the proffered envelope.

As the ticket inspector left, closing the door behind him,

Moreland opened the slim envelope and read the short message it contained.

"Well, our doppelganger has been unmasked," he informed the other two men. "Von Luck's men picked him up as soon as he stepped off the train in Brussels." Moreland smiled as he slid the note back into the envelope and tucked it away into a jacket pocket. "But they're too late by far," he added with relish.

"I would love to have seen the expression on their faces when they discovered they had been following the wrong man," laughed Templeman.

"It seems I was fortunate to catch the ferry I did," suggested Meyer-Hoffman, sounding a little unnerved.

"I can't imagine it would have made any difference," responded Moreland, relaxing back into his seat. "Your stand-in wasn't told anything about your own plans, let alone your port of departure, and Von Luck couldn't possibly have reached every port along the north coast of France before you got away. We've left them empty-handed and, no doubt, fuming."

The train was by now rattling along at a steady pace, to the accompaniment of the familiar rhythm of the clackety-clack sound the wheels made as they rode the rails. Gone were the ash-coated buildings of Portsmouth, replaced by the greenery of open fields and woodland. At one point they passed close to a road, where two men were struggling with a cart from which a wheel appeared to have broken free. A little later, they saw a fine specimen of a bull standing at the edge of a field as it watched the train pass.

Thus their journey continued for some thirty minutes or so, by which time Templeman was finding it hard to keep his eyes open, his head repeatedly dropping forward on to his chest, whereupon he would open his eyes with a start. Moreland was making some notes in a small pad he kept about his person at all times for the purpose, while Meyer-Hoffman stared out of the window, seemingly transfixed by the scenery.

This sedate scene was, however, unexpectedly disturbed when the train began to slow and then stopped. Moreland put down his notepad and pencil, then glanced out of the window.

"This doesn't look like a scheduled stop," he remarked, leaning across to get a better view. We seem to be in the middle of the countryside. Sheep and little else to be seen."

The two agents looked at one another.

"You don't think something's afoot, do you?" asked Templeman.

Moreland climbed to his feet, his face now wearing a serious look.

"Always best to assume the worst. That way you're less likely to be caught off guard. It's possible Von Luck has already been able to get a telegram through to some of his agents in this part of the country, although I would have thought that unlikely."

"We are under attack?" asked the nervous scientist, looking from one man to the other.

"Can't say for sure," replied Moreland, pulling down the blinds on the windows. "Alex, stay here with the doctor. Lock the door behind me and don't let anyone else into the compartment. I'm going to find out what's going on."

With that Moreland was gone, leaving the fidgeting scientist in the care of Templeman, who himself suddenly found his nerves a little on edge. Had they been too quick to write off Von Luck? Were things about to take a very different and dangerous turn?

AN UNEXPECTED WELCOME

It was some twelve minutes later when Templeman and Dr Meyer-Hoffman were startled by a sharp rapping on the door to the compartment. However, any thoughts of imminent danger were dispelled when the voice of Iain Moreland was heard asking them to let him in.

"False alarm," he said, as he entered, pulling the door closed behind him. "A group of sheep have escaped the confines of their field and made their way on to the line. The farmer is already here with his dog rounding up the blessed beasts. According to the guard, this sort of thing happens often on this stretch of the track. Must be some very poorly kept hedges and fencing in these parts."

There was a sigh of relief from the German, who flopped back in his seat. "That is good," he repeated to himself.

"My word, that was a tense moment and all down to nothing more than a handful of sheep," observed Templeman, who felt the tension instantly seeping from his body.

There was a little burst of laughter from the two agents, then the carriage lurched forward, stopped, then moved away again, this time picking up speed.

"That was quick work from the dog," quipped

Templeman.

Moreland pulled his pocket watch from his waistcoat pocket and checked the time.

"We'll be eighteen minutes late arriving in London, though I imagine that ought not to be long enough to go causing any great deal of alarm. Rodgers isn't the nervous sort."

"Rodgers?" enquired Meyer-Hoffman.

"Another member of the Bureau, who will be meeting us at Waterloo. He'll have a cab ready and waiting to take us to the hotel," replied Moreland.

"Ah, good," said the scientist.

As they settled back down, the train continued to pick up speed and green fields once more began to slip swiftly by.

"Doctor," began Templeman. "If you don't mind me asking, what is it about your work that makes it so very important?"

The scientist brushed at the end of one sleeve of his suit, then looked up at Templeman.

"My speciality was in developing gases to exterminate the pests and vermin that plague farmers. So many crops are lost to these animals that I found it most shocking when I discovered it is so. I believe my researches are far ahead of those of my colleagues in England and France."

"Ah, I see," said Templeman. "And all this work attracted the attention of others?"

"Yes, it is sad to report that when the Prussian military were informed of my researches and the remarkable progress I had made they decided they could use it for their own purposes. I should be clear it was never my intention that it be used by the military."

"I can quite understand your frustration, Doctor," observed Templeman. "I take it you were given no choice other than to re-direct your efforts towards military uses for your gases?"

"Quite so. The Prussian military are quite mad. They want to rule the whole world and, no doubt, the heavens too, if they can. They do everything they can to encourage the Kaiser, who is obsessed with having an empire as big as England's. I tried to refuse, but they made it very clear how unpleasant life could be for both me and my wife if I did not co-operate, so there was no choice. I did as they insisted."

"It was a shame when Bismarck left the scene," commented Moreland. "The fellow had his faults, of course, but he was remarkably sane compared to those in charge in Germany now."

"The world, it can change in an instant," observed the doctor. "We think of our kingdoms and our empires as lasting forever, but civilisations can fall in, what do you say in English? In the blink of an eye. Yes, that is it. Poof, they are gone, like that and barbarism returns to haunt the land."

"Rather pessimistic, Doctor," replied Moreland. "You sound like Alex. He too thinks we walk upon a thin veneer through which we can fall with a single wrong step, eh, Alex?"

"I do, indeed. We take these things far too much for granted."

"I tend towards a more optimistic view, myself," replied Moreland. "There always are threats to the civilised world, but so long as we are sure to keep our wits about us and for every good man to be willing to fight to defend us all against these threats, then a return to more barbaric times can be averted."

"You do not see that war is likely?" asked the scientist with a little twitch of the nose.

"It is, indeed, likely," replied Moreland. "And there are those who seem determined it should come. But I still believe that it can be avoided and I will do everything in my power to see that happens."

"That is most pleasing," came the response from Meyer-Hoffman. "Both that you should be clear to see the danger and so determined to help avoid it. I hope I too can help with this by coming here. Maybe if England gets the benefit of my researches also then the Kaiser will see his plans are hopeless."

"Well, let us hope you are right, doctor," said Templeman.

As they spoke, the train began to pass buildings once more, first a handful and then ever-growing numbers. They caught the attention of the German scientist.

"Ah, is this London, so soon?" asked Meyer-Hoffman.

Iain Moreland leaned across to better take in the scene outside.

"Yes, it looks as though we are entering the city suburbs. Another ten minutes or so and we'll be pulling into Waterloo." He glanced up at the cloud-flecked sky. "The weather's held. It looked for all the world when we set off this morning as though it would be raining by now."

"The English weather is a phenomenon indeed," said the German, smiling.

"It certainly is," responded Templeman.

*

As the three men stepped out of their carriage, they found Waterloo station to be thronging with people. It was a ceaseless hive of noisy activity. There were porters expertly loading mountains of baggage on to their trollies, whilst others were unloading, some under the watchful eye of nervous passengers. Other passengers, ones who had arrived later than planned, scurried across the concourse to reach their trains before they departed. And everywhere people struggled to make their way through the mass of bodies. Indeed, so noisy was the station that the three new arrivals were forced to raise their voices when they spoke.

Meyer-Hoffman, who had passed through the station on several previous occasions when accompanying his wife on family visits, gave the collar of his jacket a tweak and checked that his bow tie was perfectly straight.

The scientist turned to Moreland. "Where will we be finding this associate of yours? Rodgers?"

"He should be out front with a cab, waiting to take us to the hotel. We'll accompany you there, then leave you to settle in while we report to headquarters. Sir Joshua will be wanting a personal report. I expect you must be famished and ready for a good luncheon?"

"Indeed, I am. A meal will be most welcome "

They waited for an elderly couple and the porter carrying their luggage to pass them, then set off along the platform towards the exit, the scientist flanked by the two agents. However, some fifty yards or so before they reached the main concourse, and at a point where the crowd of passengers who had arrived on the train with them had begun to thin out, two men appeared as if from no where. One of them, a tall, stern-looking chap with a square jaw and sharply-angled nose, dropped in alongside Templeman, the other, a somewhat shorter though solidly built individual with narrow eyes and a thick neck, stepped in beside Moreland.

Templeman had barely noticed the close proximity of the man next to him when he felt a hard, narrow object pressed against his ribs.

"You will walk with us now or else I shoot you and Herr Doctor," growled the man into Templeman's ear. He spoke good English but the German accent was unmistakable.

"I won't.."

Templeman's complaint was cut short as the German jabbed his gun into the agent's ribs, harder this time. "You will do as you are told and walk this way in silence. Your colleague also has a gun pressed to his ribs. There is no way out for you now."

Templeman looked across at his colleague, who shook his head, warning him off trying for an escape, before speaking to Meyer-Hoffman and pointing towards a doorway that led into a long narrow building to their right. It seemed their carefully laid plans had not, after all, been good enough and that, once again, they were going to lose out to Von Luck. As they were pushed roughly through the open doorway,

Templeman felt a wave of helplessness and fear wash over him. Perhaps he wouldn't get another opportunity to settle the score with Von Luck.

BOUND TO RESPOND

The building into which they were forced was a long, narrow, single-story affair, populated for the most part with racked shelving, much of it filled with packages in all shapes and sizes. To their left was a large, solid oak workbench, on the middle of which lay a thick, worn ledger. The smell of cigarettes could just be made out and the air was chilly. Alexander Templeman also noticed that there were no windows, though there was a second door, at the far end of the building. He wondered whether it would be unlocked.

While Meyer-Hoffman had shown signs of considerable concern when he realised what was happening, Iain Moreland, Templeman noticed with admiration, had remained calm. He could see his friend carefully observing the two Germans, watching their every move; he could almost hear Moreland's mind assessing the options, calculating the odds.

Though he would be ashamed to admit it, Templeman felt no such calmness. Nor was he appraising the enemy in the same cool manner. Instead, he seemed to be somewhere between the two extremes of Moreland and Meyer-Hoffman, not yet terrified nor in full control of his senses, and he struggled to get a better grip of himself.

"I believe you English say, so near and yet so far," smirked the shorter of the two German agents, who appeared to be the more senior man. "An amusing little trip for you, Herr Doctor, but now it is time to return home, where you will answer for your treachery."

"I won't go back," stammered the scientist. "This is England and you can't force me to leave."

"Oh, but we can. We have made arrangements. You will see. Now, bring that chair here," ordered the German agent, waving his gun at a wooden chair in front of the work bench.

The chair was placed next to Templeman before the taller of the two German agents put a large, strong hand on his shoulder and pushed him down. "Sit," he snapped, before lifting a coil of rope off one of the shelves.

"You won't get far," insisted Templeman, snarling at the senior German agent. "We'll be missed soon enough and there are agents and police officers at every port in the country. You'll never escape."

The thick-necked German laughed. "There is no need to use a port to leave this stinking country. We are on an island and there are so very many places to land a boat. Even with an army of men you could not protect every beach. Now, be quiet and you, Herr Doctor, bring that other chair here."

Meyer-Hoffman hesitated, but saw something in Iain Moreland's eyes that told him to do as he was told, so he picked up the second chair and placed it as directed, next to the Scottish agent.

"Sit," ordered the German, pushing Moreland in the back with his gun.

As he did so, the handle on the door through which they had entered the building rattled loudly. Although the two German agents knew the door was now locked, they could not stop themselves from instinctively looking back to be sure.

Moreland, who had remained silent and seemingly compliant all this time, took his chance at once, knocking the gun from his opponent's hand with a swift and violent blow, then thrusting the point of one shoe into the man's nearest shin. The German cried out in pain, but still managed to catch hold of Moreland as the Scot launched himself towards the gun that now lay in the middle of the floor.

As they struggled, the taller German agent let go of the rope with which he had started to tie Templeman's hands together behind the back of the chair and grabbed his own gun from his pocket, raising it to take aim at Moreland.

Templeman struggled for all he was worth, trying his best to loosen the rope around his wrists. But, seeing at once how little chance there was of him breaking free before the German sent a volley hurtling towards his friend, he changed tack and threw himself and the chair towards the tall man.

A fraction of a second before he felt himself slam against the German agent, Templeman heard the blast of the gun being fired, the noise all but deafening so close to his ears and in such an enclosed space. There was a shout of pain from the other side of the room and then Templeman was entangled on the floor with the tall German, the Englishman flailing his legs against the other man in the desperate hope of doing some harm.

As he struggled, Templeman felt his hands come free of the knotted rope and, now up on one knee, he took a wild swing at the German as both tried to clamber up, from the floor. But the blow seemed no more than a pinprick to the bull-faced man, who merely looked at him and grinned in a manner that caused Templeman's heart to sink. It seemed the fight was a bad mismatch.

But, acting on instinct alone, Templeman saw another opportunity and, with the German standing almost upright, he swept a leg out in a wide, rapid arc and took the German's legs from under him. The tall man tumbled back to the ground, his gun spinning across the floor towards the rear of the room.

In a moment, Templeman was on his feet and about to rush for the gun when he was stopped in his tracks by a shout from the second German agent.

"Stop or I shoot your friend," he barked.

Templeman froze, then turned to see the German pointing his gun at Moreland, who lay on the ground holding his right shoulder, blood seeping between his fingers. From the look of anguish on his face it was clear he was in considerable pain. Templeman let his arms drop to his sides.

"A very noble effort, gentlemen," said the shorter German, breathing a little heavily and a dark bruise already showing on his left cheek where the bone was close to the surface. "But enough of these games…" He broke off, looking quizzically towards the rear of the room.

Templeman was about to turn his head to follow the German's gaze when there was a violent explosion from the front of the building as the door was almost smashed off its hinges, splinters flying in all directions.

The tall, burly figure of Rogers, wrapped in a long grey coat appeared in the doorway. Even before he had fully entered the room, he let loose two shots from his revolver, both aimed at the taller German agent. The first split the wooden shelving above the German's shoulder, but the second slammed into his upper arm. Templeman felt a ripple of pleasure as he heard the man curse.

The shorter German spun round and let off two shots of his own, but Rodgers was already moving low and fast down the right-hand side of the room and the bullets thudded harmlessly into the wall.

There was a brief shouted exchange between the two Germans before they fired a flurry of bullets at the closing Rodgers, then fled towards the rear door. As they tumbled though the open doorway, three more bullets from Rodgers crashed into the door frame and then the two Germans were gone.

Rodgers cursed his poor aim, but Templeman felt nothing other than blessed relief, his heart beating rapidly in his chest and sweat trickling down both temples. That had been the nearest of near misses.

"Thank Heavens for your arrival, Rodgers," he managed

to get out, in between deep breaths. "I thought we were done for."

Rodgers holstered his weapon and stepped towards the ailing Moreland. "When I saw how late you were, I came into the station to see if someone might be able to tell me what was happening. That was fortunate because it meant I heard the gun fire. It didn't seem likely there would be any other reason for someone to be firing a gun, so I assumed you must be in some sort of trouble."

He helped Moreland to his feet and righted the nearest of the chairs for the wounded man to sit on.

"Well, it's a good job you did because I doubt the outcome would have been favourable to us otherwise," said Templeman as he reached out to pick up the second chair.

"The doctor," interceded Moreland through the pain burning in his arm. "Where is Meyer-Hoffman?"

Templeman let go of his grip on the chair and looked around the room. "That's a very good question," he remarked. "Doctor, are you hiding somewhere? The German agents have fled. Rodgers saw them off," he called out.

Still there was no sign of the scientist.

"Rodgers, you take that side of the room and I will take this side," instructed Templeman, as he began to move from one section of shelving to another.

It took less than a minute for the two men to complete their search and when it was done Templeman informed the ailing Moreland of the outcome. "There's no sign of him, I'm afraid. He's gone. That's for certain. But what isn't certain is whether he left on his own or as a prisoner of our two German friends."

"Let us hope it was the former," said Moreland, his voice tired and tinged with pain. "I doubt we'll get another chance to free him from the hands of Von Luck and his colleagues if they have seized him."

The Sultan of Zanzire

WELCOME NEWS

The atmosphere in Sir Joshua's office was glum. Sir Joshua, himself, seated behind his desk fiddling with his pipe, seemingly unable to decide whether to re-fill it and light up or use it to rap impatiently against the woodwork. He'd not said a word to Alexander Templeman since Vivian Eastwood had left the room to get an update on Iain Moreland, who had been taken to London's St Thomas' Hospital, on the point of passing out after such a heavy loss of blood. That had been a little over an hour ago.

Sir Joshua had greeted them curtly when they responded to his summons and Templeman had decided it would be best if he spoke only when requested to do so. However, whereas he had initially thought Sir Joshua's greatest concern would be with regard to the disappearance of Dr Meyer-Hoffman, it had quickly become clear that the Head of the Bureau was, initially at least, primarily concerned for the health of his wounded agent. Templeman wondered if the same would be true of Von Luck in similar circumstances. He considered it unlikely.

"Damned mess," barked Sir Joshua, seemingly more to the room than to Templeman.

The younger man shifted in his chair. "Indeed," he said.

Sir Joshua placed his pipe on the desk, then pulled out his pocketwatch. Only two minutes had passed since he'd last done the same thing. He put the watch back in his waistcoat pocket and picked his pipe up, tapping it on the edge of the desk before pushing it between his lips.

As he did so, the door swept open and Vivian Eastwood returned, swinging the door shut behind him.

"Well?" demanded Sir Joshua before Eastwood had even had time to sit down.

"He's going to pull through," replied Eastwood, sounding a little breathless. "Lost a lot of blood, but the doctor says the bullet came out cleanly. No complications. Told us not to worry in the slightest."

"Not to worry," scoffed Sir Joshua, waving his pipe in the air. "Easy for him to say. Not responsible for the fellow. In any case, that's welcome news. Can't abide losing an agent. A risk you all run, I know that, but doesn't make it any easier for me to accept. Now then, what about these two German agents, do we know who they are and where they've gone to ground?"

Eastwood shook his head. "Other than the descriptions Templeman, Moreland and Rodgers were able to provide us with we know nothing about them. Either they're newly placed here or they've been keeping their heads down, until now. We've got all our own people on the look out for them and, of course, Scotland Yard are after them too, but not a sign so far."

"Think they could have reached the German Embassy before we were in position to intercept them?"

"It's possible," replied Eastwood, "Though I'm not sure that would have been their best course of action. If they do have Meyer-Hoffman, they'd all be trapped in the Embassy, unable to transport him back to Germany. I would have thought it more likely they've either made straight for a port, somewhere quiet and out of the way, or some secret, temporary residence where they can hide out while things blow over."

"What do you think to that, Templeman?" asked Sir Joshua.

The junior man had not been expecting to be asked for his opinion and for a moment he was caught off balance. "I've precious little experience of these things, of course, but I agree, returning to the Embassy wouldn't seem the wisest of moves. If I was them, I'd make straight for the nearest port and embark as quickly as possible."

Sir Joshua eyed the other two men closely for a moment.

"What if I told you they don't have Meyer-Hoffman? How might that change things?"

Eastwood, who had slumped somewhat in his chair, sat up with a jolt. "Are you merely speculating, Sir Joshua? Or have you received fresh intelligence?"

"Shortly before I summoned the two of you here, I received a phone call from Dr Meyer-Hoffman. The poor chap sounded terrified, which I suppose is not entirely without good reason, given the circumstances of the events at Waterloo station. He confirmed that he got away from the station before the German agents were able to snatch him and he's unscathed, physically at least."

"Excellent news," responded Eastwood, smacking a hand on the arm of his chair.

"Not such a dismal situation as we feared," chipped in Templeman, sounding as he felt, rather more upbeat.

"Indeed not," replied Sir Joshua. "Along with the news from the hospital, that's two very welcome developments."

"Did he say where he's staying?" asked Eastwood.

"That was information he was unwilling to divulge, although more about that shortly. He did, though, also confirm he has possession of his briefcase."

"That's good to hear," said Eastwood, with obvious relief. "If the worst should yet happen to the doctor, at least we could anticipate getting our hands on his papers. That would leave our own scientists in a sound enough spot to benefit from his work."

"Better that we keep Meyer-Hoffman alive so that he can

continue with his researches himself," replied Sir Joshua, raising an eyebrow. "But it is a tad frustrating that the man refuses to let us know where he's staying."

"In which case, what do we do next?" asked Templeman, rubbing a hand across his chin,

"That has already been decided by the doctor," answered the Head of the Bureau, his tone betraying a sense of unease. "It seems he has some familiarity with the little town of Rye. It's down on the Sussex coast. One of the old Cinque Ports. Apparently he's stayed there with his wife on two occasions and it seems it meets the double criteria of being both sufficiently familiar and safely quiet enough for the doctor to decide that is where he will look to lie low, until we've sorted out the mess here."

"You don't sound awfully convinced?" prompted Eastwood.

"Would much rather have the chap locked up somewhere safe and sound with half-a-dozen of our agents here in London. But he's not for anything of the sort, so we'll just have to go along with his scheme and hope for the best."

"But we'll be sending agents down to Rye, I take it?" asked Eastwood.

"Agent," replied Sir Joshua, with the emphasis on the singular.

A quizzical look appeared on Eastwood's face. "A single agent?" he asked, sounding incredulous.

"I'm afraid so. Again, it's at Meyer-Hoffman's insistence," replied Sir Joshua, turning his gaze on Templeman. "It seems that you, Templeman, and Moreland made rather a good impression on the doctor, because he was hoping Moreland would be up to the job of acting as bodyguard, until I made it plain that was out of the question. Fortunately, he agreed to allow you to join him, instead. But it must be you alone. It seems the good doctor has determined both that it's not safe to be seen in public in this vast metropolis of ours and that he is best off minimising the number of people he has contact with."

"That's quite the compliment," observed Templeman. "I hope I can repay the doctor's faith. I'd hate to let him down after all he's been through."

"Indeed and I can't emphasise enough how important this is to us," said Sir Joshua, his tone turning somewhat stern. "If we were to lose Meyer-Hoffman and his papers it would set back our attempts to catch up with the German's development of chemical weapons no end. In all likelihood we would still be lagging by the time war commences and the consequences of that could be disastrous. That's quite the burden for you to bear, Templeman, but I wouldn't have agreed to it in the first place if I didn't absolutely believe you to be up to the job."

"Quite so," chipped in Eastwood, nodding his head.

"I appreciate your words of support," replied Templeman. "Both of you. Of course, I'll do everything in my power to keep Dr Meyer-Hoffman safe." Templeman paused briefly before adding, "But, is there any chance that Von Luck might become aware of the doctor's plans? After all, he soon worked out that we were bringing him up to London from Portsmouth."

"I would like to think not, but it's no doubt best to approach things on the assumption that the opposition will find out sooner or later," responded Sir Joshua. "At least then you are less likely to get caught out."

"Do we know where Meyer-Hoffman intends to stay when he reaches Rye?" asked Templeman, his mind racing on to practical matters.

"Not as yet," replied the Head of the Bureau. "He will let me know once he has found somewhere suitable to stay. Apparently there are two or three hotels in the town that cater for the holidaying visitors that travel to the town in the summer months. He might, though, choose somewhere less obvious. I'll inform you as soon as I hear again from him."

"It seems we can't keep you away from a good adventure, Templeman," remarked Eastwood, the hint of a smile on his face. "I'm really rather jealous."

"Well, you did warn me about such things when I agreed to join the Bureau. I suppose I can't complain about a lack of excitement in my life."

"Well, let's hope this one goes as well as the others," chipped in Sir Joshua.

"But what I can't work out," began Eastwood, sounding serious once more. "Is how the devil Von Luck knew about Meyer-Hoffman's escape route and his intended arrival at Waterloo. And to know soon enough to be able to get two of his agents in place ready to make an interception. His network and communications channels here must be far more developed than we've believed to be the case up until now."

"It seems so," replied Sir Joshua. "The chap must have got a message through to his agents here as soon as they realised the man they'd been duped into following to Brussels wasn't Meyer-Hoffman. Von Luck must have been able to deploy agents to every major railway terminus in London, which, if true, would point to them being here in far larger numbers than we'd thought."

"Surely that would amount to a small army?" suggested Templeman, sounding almost incredulous.

"Well, either Von Luck has the men here to deploy in such numbers," replied Eastwood. "Or else he made some quick assumptions about entry ports and which railway stations were the most likely to need covering. But either way, he was able to move with remarkable speed. It's really rather concerning. I'm not at all certain we could respond like that should the positions be reversed."

"Indeed," began Sir Joshua, getting to his feet and stepping across to the window as he spoke. "But we'll need to put such matters to one side for now. As things stand, our priority is to get you, Templeman, to Rye, where you can attend to the doctor's safety, while we set about the task of dealing with these German agents, if they've not already fled back home. Now then, Eastwood, you'd better arrange for us to pay a visit at Scotland Yard. I'm sure that Commissioner

Albert Tellerman will appreciate us g_ving him a personal update on the matter."

"A sound idea, sir. I'll get on to it right away."

As Sir Joshua brought his hands together behind his back, the other two men stood up, ready to depart.

"Templeman, if you don't mind, I'd like a word before you leave."

"Of course, Sir Joshua."

A SHOCKING SECRET

As soon as the door was closed behind the departing Vivian Eastwood, Sir Joshua stepped swiftly back to his desk, laying his pipe on the broad oak surface. His face wore a look of concern and Templeman observed an eagerness in Sir Joshua's manner that he couldn't recall having seen before.

"Couldn't share this with you while there were others present," began Sir Joshua in a low, conspiratorial voice, the fingers of one hand playing along the edge of his desk. "Like you, I was astonished that Von Luck was able to move his agents into place quickly enough to intercept you at Waterloo. Seemed a quite remarkable effort to me. The man must have had everything in place beforehand, ready for an eventuality of the sort, as well as a communications channel second to none."

The older man looked down at his desk then back up at Templeman, who waited in silence, uncertain where the conversation was heading.

"But there's another explanation," continued Sir Joshua, his manner hesitant. "You see, I have for some time been concerned that we might have a traitor in our midst."

Templeman couldn't stop the astonishment he felt showing on his face. "Good Lord," he said, barely able to believe the idea possible. "But who? Why?"

"Well, those are the key questions to ask. Unfortunately, I don't have the answers. But what I do know is that, since the early part of last year, there have been a number of minor incidents. Coincidences, you could say. Operations that haven't quite turned out as had been expected. Not complete disasters, you understand. Just a few, though significant, shortcomings that meant we didn't achieve all we set out to. Then word got back to me at the beginning of this year that the Germans knew about a select, high-level conference we were planning to hold with our French counterparts. Looking for ways we could better work together, that sort of thing. The information could have leaked from France, of course, but coming, as it did, on the back of all these other peculiar incidents of bad luck, I concluded it more likely the information had come from here."

The very act of sharing his suspicions with Templeman took some of the weight he'd been carrying off Sir Joshua's shoulders and he felt the tension within him ease a little. The old proverb about a burden shared came to mind as he eased himself down into his chair, comforted further by its familiar embrace.

"I decided last month it was time to undertake a minor, clandestine operation of my own," he went on, leaning forward, his arms resting on the desk. "I drew up some supposedly secret papers setting out a proposal for re-organising the Bureau, then left them on my desk the following weekend after dropping a few hints to several people. I did consider having the place put under surveillance by Scotland Yard, but I'd no desire to share my concerns at that stage and, in any case, I couldn't be entirely certain Von Luck doesn't have spies operating there as well."

"Astonishing," remarked Templeman, still barely able to believe what he was hearing.

"Quite," replied Sir Joshua. "So, I left things at that. When I returned to the Bureau on the Monday morning everything appeared to be in order. No sign of anyone having let themselves into this office and the papers were still here, on this desk. But, low and behold, a fortnight later I received word from our agent in the German secret service saying that they seemed to be aware of my plans for re-organising the Bureau and were busy considering their response."

"So, there's no doubt about it; there is a traitor at work here," said Templeman, running a hand across the back of his head.

"It would seem so. I declared myself unhappy with the proposed changes to the Bureau, so as not to arouse any suspicion by failing to proceed with implementing them. The trouble I then faced, as I'm sure you can appreciate, was how to go about unmasking the traitor. Given the timeframe, the only people I confidently feel able to trust are those, like yourself, who have joined us no more recently than, say, last Easter. Which, in fact, means there's just you and Ridgway-Hart who are in the clear and neither of you have the experience to deal with such a tricky situation. No insult intended, Templeman. Just a realistic appraisal of things."

"None taken, Sir Joshua. You're absolutely right and Ridgway-Hart is an even less experienced agent than am I."

"Indeed, he is."

"So, what did you decide?"

"Nothing for it. Since it wasn't possible to have the spies investigating the spies, I had no choice but to speak to Tellerman at the Yard. All in private, of course."

"Albert Tellerman, eh? I've yet to meet the man myself."

"That's right. We've known each other a long time. Rather caustic sort, but excellent at his job. He agreed it looks as though Von Luck has a man on the inside. Felt a little aggrieved I hadn't taken him into my confidence sooner, but appreciated my desire to be certain of things before raising the matter with him."

"And were the two of you able to come up with some scheme to unmask this traitor?" asked Templeman.

"We both acknowledged it will be a tricky business, all the

more so if we want to apprehend this individual before they get the chance to flee. And, rest assured, that's very much what we want to do. I won't be happy until I get to see this fellow swinging from the end of a rope. Tellerman had an idea or two in mind, but our agreed plan has only this week been put into operation. There's no way of knowing how long it will be until we're successful and, in the meantime, agents such as yourself will have to continue operating while the opposition holds an ace in their hand."

Templeman puffed out his cheeks and took a couple of steps towards the window as he weighed up what he had been told.

"So, that's how Von Luck got those two agents in place at Waterloo?"

"It would seem so, yes," replied Sir Joshua, leaning back in his chair, his pipe back in his hand.

"And I suppose it's possible he'll know soon enough that Meyer-Hoffman plans to lie low in Rye?"

"That's why I wanted to speak to you now. I felt it important that you are aware there is every possibility Von Luck will find out about that. It may not be a pleasant thought, but I suggest you approach this assignment on the assumption there will be German agents in the town soon enough. I'd like you to draw a hand gun from the armoury before you go. After the incident at Waterloo, it's clear enough the Germans have no hesitation in both carrying and using weapons, so you need to be armed yourself."

"Yes, of course."

Templeman felt a deep sense of unease at this news. Not only that he could expect there to be German agents in Rye, but that he may be forced into an armed confrontation with them. He'd had all the usual training when he joined the Bureau, of course, but he was no sharp shooter and guns felt awkward and uncomfortable in his hand. As for the idea of shooting another man; well, he would do it in the service of King and country, but the notion left a bad taste in his mouth.

"Right then, let's not keep you here any longer than needs be," said Sir Joshua. "A room has been booked for you at the Queen Charlotte Hotel in Rye. Pleasant place, I'm given to understand, though don't know it myself." There was a pause before Sir Joshua continued. "There's only one priority for you here, Templeman, and that is to keep Dr Meyer-Hoffman safe and out of the hands of Von Luck. All other considerations are of no consequence, is that clear?"

"Absolutely, Sir Joshua."

"Only contact me in extremis. It's too risky for you to be making reports to this office, given the circumstances. If we're able to track down this blasted traitor in the next few days, I will get a message to you and we can make arrangements for the safe return of the doctor to London and the happy embrace of his wife."

"And if you can't identify the traitor in the next few days, what will we do then?" asked Templeman.

"We'll have to come up with some other scheme for tucking the doctor and his wife safely away, somewhere Von Luck can't get at them. I've an idea or two on that front, but we'll fall back on those when the time comes. For now, you concentrate on keeping Meyer-Hoffman in one piece and in our hands."

"You can count on me, sir. I'll do whatever needs to be done to keep the doctor out of the grasp of Von Luck."

"I hope so, Templeman, because right now I'm not sure who else I can trust to do the job."

The Sultan of Zanzire

A PRETTY LITTLE TOWN

The afternoon train journey south from London had been a pleasant one. Alexander Templeman had sat alone by the large window of his compartment, basking in the pleasing embrace of a gently warming sun, as the train passed through one picturesque scene after another. Here a shadow-filled woodland populated with oak and chestnut, birch and hazel. Next wide open pasture, neatly parcelled up by endless miles of hedgerow, or a bare field in which the first green shoots of wheat or barley could be seen emerging into the light. It had warmed his heart and filled his soul with joy to see such sights as England had to offer and thereby added to his determination that Von Luck would not snatch Meyer-Hoffman from out of his hands.

Changing trains at Ashford, Templeman had found himself completing the last, shorter leg of his journey in the company of a mother and her young daughter, who were on their way to visit relatives in Hastings. The daughter, who could not have been more than six or perhaps seven years of age, had been tremendously excited at the prospect of once more setting eyes on the sea and had expressed an ardent desire, not shared by her mother, to get her feet wet in the endless waves. These she described, much to Templeman's amusement, as being toe-ticklers.

It had been something of a disappointment to say farewell to the daughter in particular when they arrived at Rye railway station, where it seemed he was one of only two passengers to alight. As if greeting his arrival on the coast, a squadron of seagulls swept overhead, their shrill cries cutting through the sky and Templeman found a lightness and freshness to the air that was in marked contrast to what he had left behind in London.

Templeman had walked the short distance from the modest, little railway station to the Queen Charlotte Hotel, which he found towards the northern end of the High Street, high on a bluff that overlooked the vast expanse of Walland Marsh. The hotel was primarily a rather attractive Georgian affair, all red brick and neatly proportioned panelled windows, though at one end a mid-Victorian addition looked ugly and unwelcome by comparison. Inside the hotel, the carpets were a little too worn and there was a vague, almost distant smell of mustiness. But, such minor shortcomings aside, the Queen Charlotte seemed pleasant enough and the greeting he received from the well-dressed and attentive receptionist was warm and professional.

Although there had been no prior agreement on the matter, Templeman had wondered if, upon checking in, he might find there was already a note awaiting him from Meyer-Hoffman. It was easy to imagine the man would be desperately keen to welcome the protection that Templeman offered. But there was nothing of the sort and the man from the Bureau couldn't help feeling a little deflated when he discovered this to be the case.

He had been assigned a room at the front of the hotel, with a view over the High Street and out across the marshland to the east. The bed was a little too soft, though bearable, and he thought perhaps the décor in the room had not been updated for two decades or more. He did, however, also notice there was a loose, squeaking floorboard in the corridor a yard or so before the doorway to his room. That might at least give him a little warning of anyone approaching and could prove vital should Von Luck's agents track him down and come looking to cause mischief.

Having unpacked his luggage and acquainted himself with the amenities offered by the hotel, Templeman decided he would like to get to know the town. For one thing, it looked a pretty sight and, for another, it would be wise of him to know the lie of the land, especially if there should be any need to move quickly and with little warning. As a man of the intelligence service, it would be unforgivable not to furnish himself with such knowledge.

The receptionist had pointed out some of the primary attractions the town had to offer and Templeman started with the first of these, the fourteenth-century Landgate that had once been the northern point of access into the town. It now stood alone, its adjoining walls long since vanished. It was, though, still the main route out of Rye for those travelling northwards or, as he imagined he would do, should an opportunity present itself, for those wishing to enjoy the hiking opportunities that lay inland.

From there, he retraced his steps back past the Queen Charlotte Hotel and on along the High Street. A busy commercial thoroughfare that appeared to be doing good business, there were many people for Templeman to thread his way between. The buildings were mostly of red brick construction, some with wooden facias, and all seemed to be topped off with red tiled roofs. It seemed that stone of any sort was in short supply in the area, for very few buildings were made of it.

Here and there narrow roads led off to either side, those to his left running up the the hill on which the town was built, while those to his right rolling away downhill to another road that skirted the foot of the slope and what remained of the old town wall.

It was, he contemplated, a pretty little town that belonged to a period in time long left behind and it was easy to see why people were drawn to see its beauty. Under other circumstances, he would have been happy to relax in its welcoming and comforting embrace for a day or two. But on this occasion he was there on more serious business and his exploration was not recreational in nature; rather it was to seek out information that might prove useful.

After a while, having confused himself and taken a wrong turn, he found himself overlooking a small quay on the River Tillingham, which arced around the bottom of the town before spilling into the River Rother. Although modest in size, the quay was busy, small boats moored against a wooden jetty on the town side, others beached on the narrow, gently sloping sandbank opposite. Men with beards and grizzled faces, almost all of whom seemed to have a pipe or cigarette fixed firmly between their teeth, were busy about their business of unloading or loading cargo.

The shouts of the men mingled with the cries of gulls, which were everywhere, their sharp eyes looking for any opportunity, while the salt-laced smell of the sea filled Templeman's nostrils. He placed a hand on a stretch of worn wooden railing and found it coated with an unpleasantly sticky green slime that must have been fed by the winds and the sea over the course of decades.

As he stood there observing, Templeman had the thought that the quay would make a fine point of entry for Von Luck's agents, should they wish to avoid arriving in the town by the more obvious means of the railway line. Indeed, it also offered a clear means of escape to the Channel and onwards to Germany, should the agents manage to snatch away Meyer-Hoffman. Such a clear point of departure caused him some unease, but there was precious little he could do about the matter right then, other than bear it in mind.

Leaving behind the shouts of the sailors and the cries of the gulls, Templeman turned back towards the town centre, this time making his way up Mermaid Street, as pretty a little cobbled lane as a man could ever hope to see. It led uphill to the thirteenth-century St Mary's Church, with its little graveyard of sombre headstones. Templeman had briefly considered taking a look inside the church, but there was another nearby building that he was especially keen to see, so he continued on his way, taking a road towards the south-eastern extremities of the town.

Rye Castle, which he had been informed was known more readily by the town's residents as Ypres Tower, sat above the cliffs overlooking the point at which the Tillingham joined the Rother. It was a splendid, if rather small, stone castle built during the fourteenth-century and Templeman spent a short while perusing the fortifications.

Once his curiosity had been satisfied, the man from the Bureau navigated a short series of steps that led down to a simple garden between the Tower and the cliff's edge. He found himself to be the only person there, his sole company the ever-present gulls arcing across the sky and the chill, salt-laden wind that was gusting in fitfully from the English Channel.

He buttoned his coat and pulled the collar up around his neck before turning to look out towards the east and the vast, flat, unwelcoming expanse of Walland Marsh, where water-filled dykes divided up fields of grass on which grazed a particularly hardy breed of sheep. Angling away to his right was the mud-banked Rother, which emptied into the Channel two miles or so further on, past the small fishing fleet and a cluster of other boats that were moored or sitting at anchor adjacent to a small hamlet.

The sight before him looked to Templeman to be an entirely other world; one that bore no relationship to the safe, civilised one in which he currently stood. It left him with an unexpected and unpleasant sense of foreboding, as if the immense and unwelcoming marshy expanse had some significant part to play in his near future. He shivered, as a particularly strong gust of wind whistled across the cliff top, then took one last look at the view, and turned to begin the walk back to the Queen Charlotte.

ENQUIRIES AFTER GERMAN VISITORS

Templeman had thought it a possibility that, with the town being so small and tightly-packed, he might be lucky enough to bump into Meyer-Hoffman during the course of his explorations. Not only had that failed to materialise, there was also still no message from the scientist when he got back to the hotel.

Reminding himself of the need to remain patient, Templeman enjoyed a late luncheon in the hotel dining room before settling down with a pot of tea to begin perusing a map he had purchased from a stationers on his way back from the Ypres Tower that showed the town and the surrounding area. The more he knew of the place, the better prepared he would be for any possible eventuality, a notion that had only been underlined by the peculiar sense of foreboding he had felt looking out at the marsh.

Perhaps, he mused, his unease was simply down to the fact he was there all alone and his mission was a vital one. It was only reasonable, under such circumstances, that he should feel a certain degree of discomfort and concern; all the more so given his relative inexperience as an agent. Ah, what he wouldn't have given for Iain Moreland to be there with him; to guide him through this quagmire of challenges.

But there was no use moping; he was on his own and that was an end to the matter.

*

Having enjoyed the luxury of an afternoon nap, Templeman had washed and changed into fresh clothes before returning to the hotel dining room a little after six. He ate an acceptable dinner of lamb cutlets which, the waiter assured him, were from animals that had been fattened on the very marshland he had been surveying earlier in the day.

His frequent enquiries at reception had already clearly established an identified routine amongst the staff, for he had not even opened his mouth on this occasion when he was informed there was still no message for him. He smiled at the predictability of his approach and assured the receptionist that he would leave at least one whole hour between his enquiries in future.

Having tried and failed to then relax with the day's newspapers in the hotel lounge, where repetitious conversation between three elderly ladies became something of an irritating distraction, Templeman decided to take another stroll along the High Street. He thought perhaps it might present itself in a different light given it was now a little after seven-thirty and the sun had long since dropped over the western horizon.

Although wrapped up tightly in his coat, Templeman still felt the chill of the evening air and it quickly livened up his senses, which he considered was certainly no bad thing. There were few other people about and those who were seemed intent on retreating to the warmth of their homes as quickly as their feet could get them there.

Gas light flickered in windows as he passed them and the air was laced with the smell of smoke from hearth fires. At one point, as he reached the darkened premises of a grocer, a scruffy cat emerged from behind a cart wheel and paused to look up at him with great suspicion before strolling across the street and disappearing through a narrow gap in a stone wall.

And then, just as he was beginning to ask himself where he might find something of interest, Templeman came to the Red Lion Inn. He had barely noticed it during his daylight walk along the High Street, when it had been forced to compete for his attention alongside a myriad of other attractions. But now, with the neighbouring shops closed and silent and the street almost deserted, its flickering lights stood out in the darkness like beacons and the noise of many boisterous conversations reached Templeman's ears.

As if the temptation to enter the inn was not already great enough, as he stood looking in through one of the large panelled windows, a thought occurred to him. Did this, he asked himself, not only offer the prospect of a pleasant way to spend the evening, but also present him with an opportunity to do a little casual intelligence gathering?

Perhaps those inside, their tongues loosened by beer, would feel freer than usual about talking to a stranger and give him the chance to ask questions that might seem a little impertinent at other times. Feeling altogether more lively now he had a purpose in mind, Templeman stepped jauntily into the warm embrace of the inn.

The premises were, in fact, busier even than they had appeared from outside. Indeed, it seemed as though half the men of the town might be there. The air was thick with pipe and cigarette smoke and the noise of a dozen or more conversations, some of them exceedingly lively and interspersed with laughter, assaulted his ears. It was a stark and welcome contrast with the near deserted and silent lounge of the Queen Charlotte.

He bought himself a pint of ale from the wiry old barmaid and found a seat at a small round table in a window bay that looked out on to the High Street, well away from the enormous log fire that burned in a vast fireplace at the far end of the room. A great roar went up from a group of half a dozen men standing at the far end of the bar. What its cause was, Templeman could not make out.

After perhaps ten minutes, as more customers joined the noisy throng, two elderly and newly arrived gentlemen, in search of somewhere to sit, enquired about the unoccupied chairs around Templeman's table. Pleased by their arrival, Templeman gave them every encouragement to join him.

"Chilly out this evening," observed Templeman, as the two men took their seats.

"Ah, 'tis nothing," replied the man to his right, a large, portly fellow with a fleshy face whose small, round glasses sat uneasily on his bulbous nose. "The winter was bad this year. Had snow three feet deep in the street out there and the temperature got so low I thought I might freeze to death in my bed."

"You like your bed too much as it is," said the second man, a short, thin individual with a thick mop of greying hair and big, bushy eyebrows. Templeman also noticed that he had unusually long fingers that were able to wrap almost all the way around his tankard.

"I'm not so young any more," replied the larger man, his voice deep and gravelly. "Man my age likes his bed more and more with each passing year. I suppose that's where Sarah will find me one morning, cold as could be and no longer of this world."

The two men laughed and swallowed a deep draught of their beer.

"You live in Rye?" asked Templeman, beginning his attempt to steer the conversation towards some useful topic.

"That we do," answered the thin man. "Gilchrist here, he owns the tobacconists down the road a ways, on the Mint. Been there, what, twenty years or above, have you?" he asked his friend.

"Twenty-four this summer," replied Gilchrist. "Seems as if I opened the shop not longer ago than last year. Time's a funny thing."

"That's eight more years than I've owned the stationers up the road there," said the thin man.

"Smith and Taylors?" asked Templeman.

"That's the one. There is no Smith these days. He left this earth seven years back. Just me now, George Taylor."

"Ah, I purchased a map of the town from your store only this morning," said Templeman. "There was another chap behind the counter then. Tall fellow, with a large nose."

"That would be my son, Albert. He's hoping to take on the business just as soon as he can."

"He's too eager, if you ask me," laughed Gilchrist. "He'll have you falling down a set of stairs or getting run over by a cart one of these days, you mark my words."

"Young folk, they're too keen. Don't know how many years it takes to acquire the skills a man needs to run a business," observed Taylor.

"You're here to take in the sights, then?" asked Gilchrist of Templeman.

"I am, indeed. Staying at the Queen Charlotte."

"Could do worse," commented Taylor as he brought his tankard up to his mouth.

"Seems a pleasant enough place," responded Templeman. "I was recommended a visit to the town and a stay at the Queen Charlotte by a friend of mine in London. Been down here several times himself. Insisted it's as pretty a little town as you're ever likely to see and I must say he seems to be right about that."

"True enough," said Gilchrist, shifting awkwardly in his chair. "We're fortunate in that respect. The place hasn't been knocked around overly much in more recent times. Not like Hastings. Some nasty looking buildings gone up there."

There was another roar of laughter from the group of men at the far end of the bar.

"That's old Adams," said Taylor as Templeman looked up. "He tells the tallest tales a man ever did hear. Where he gets them from, the Lord only knows."

"And half of them are so rude that he'd not be able to repeat them outside of a place like this," added Gilchrist.

"Tellers of tales are always popular people," replied

Templeman. "It's the finest form of entertainment, I always think."

There was a pause in the conversation as a short-lived burst of song came from the group at the bar.

"I suppose you get a good many visitors from overseas," observed Templeman, steering the conversation back on course. "The friend I mentioned is German, though he's lived in London for several years and has a Scottish wife. He tells me he's encountered other Germans here on some of his visits. Have you met any Germans here yourself?"

"Never the one of 'em," replied Gilchrist, scratching at an ear with a chubby hand. "Had a Frenchman in the store last week. Strange fellow. Thought I'd sell the same tobacco as he buys in Calais, as if I'd stock inferior quality products like that. Sold him a pouch of my own mix, not that he looked all that happy at it. Never saw him again."

"Always getting French people in my store," said Taylor. "They come for the postcards mostly. I keep telling Albert that he should learn the language, as it would be good for business, but he shows no interest. Had a German in the store a few weeks back. I remember him because he looked a bit like the Kaiser and his wife went round the store looking down her nose at everything. Mind you, I shouldn't complain. The man bought twenty postcards."

Templeman felt a little deflated by his companions' replies, having hoped they might have received custom from a man with a likeness to Meyer-Hoffman. He made an effort at describing the scientist's appearance to them in the hope they might recall a recent sighting, but that too brought a disappointing reply.

"Are you one of those types that likes to walk all over the countryside?" asked Gilchrist, as the conversation returned to the nature of Templeman's stay. He sounded unimpressed at the idea.

"I do indeed intend to get plenty of exercise during my stay," replied Templeman with enthusiasm. "Long walks are my thing. Are there any routes you'd recommend a fellow to take? Good views and an inn along the way for luncheon would be very welcome."

"I'd stay away from the Marsh," replied Taylor. "Filled with dykes and quicksands, it is. A man can soon enough find himself trapped in that maze of hazards. Foul weather blows up out of nowhere too. If I was you, I'd take one of the old trackways inland. Tenterden is a pleasant enough place and the old Pheasant Inn does a hearty meal. You could walk there and back in a day."

"But you'll not be walking in those clothes, now, will you?" asked Gilchrist, running an eye over Templeman's attire.

The agent smiled. "Absolutely not. I have my walking boots and proper outdoors clothes back at the hotel. I've done quite a bit of walking in the Scottish Lowlands and I'm very familiar with how quickly the weather can close in on a man."

"That it can," said Taylor before swallowing the last of his beer.

The three men continued their conversation for a while longer, the two shopkeepers making a passable effort at addressing Templeman's deficiency in knowledge of the town's history and the vital role it had played in seeing off the threat from France in centuries past. Indeed, it seemed as if they felt such times had occurred only very recently and there remained a menacing threat from the country on the other side of the English Channel. In a way, that was very true, considered Templeman, except that it was Germany and not France that was now the coming foe.

Templeman did, however, also learn that the nature of the tides in the area was such that each day offered only a very few hours during which a boat of any meaningful size could be moved in and out of the small quay he had visited on his earlier walk through the town. That substantially narrowed the window of opportunity open to von Luck's men should they be planning to take a boat from there out to the sea; a limitation that might prove crucial should matters take a turn for the worse. It was precisely the kind of useful information that the man from the Bureau had been hoping to pick up from his new acquaintances and it seemed a good reward for his efforts.

Eventually, as the evening moved on towards ten o'clock, Templeman extricated himself from the grip of the other men's conversation and walked back out into the chilly night, the cloudless sky sparkling with countless stars. He stood in the street for a while, breathing in the fresh salt-tinged air and listened to the night, the silence broken only by the sounds that leaked from the establishment behind him. It was a far cry from London, where silence was an almost unknown commodity and fogs were often so ghastly thick they were a danger to one's health.

The call of an owl from amongst the trees in the churchyard broke his contemplation of the evening and, buttoning up the collar of his coat, he set off towards the hotel, intent on being early to bed so he would wake fully refreshed for what might become a demanding day.

*

Once again, Templeman found no message waiting for him when he got back to the Queen Charlotte, though the alcohol he had consumed left him feeling somewhat more relaxed about the matter than previously.

He let himself into his room, where a small gaslight cast a soft glow. Almost at once, Templeman felt uneasy. It wasn't something he could put his finger on, but there was definitely something wrong. He stood in the middle of the room and looked about the place with a studied care, but nothing stood out to explain his sense of unease.

Stepping across to the large oak wardrobe, he opened the door and peered inside at his small collection of clothes hanging there. It took a moment, but then he realised what was wrong and with a growing sense of urgency he moved across to the single chest of drawers. Opening the top drawer, the only one he had made use of, he found the same outcome. And, finally, as he looked once more at his recently acquired map and his small notepad, that both sat on top of the chest of drawers, he realised what was wrong.

They were only small things, but they said all that needed saying. The clothes in both the wardrobe and the chest of drawers, as well as the map and notepad, were too neatly arranged. Although not a messy person, he was not obsessive about such things. There was no doubt about it, his room had been searched.

THE FIRST MORNING

Templeman breakfasted on scrambled eggs and bacon, with a pot of piping hot tea, in the fine if slightly tired Georgian dining room that looked out across the High Street to the flatness of the marsh, away to the east. However, despite the quality of the food and eagerness of his appetite, he had not been able to relax and enjoy his meal.

The discovery of the evening before had made for a fitful night's sleep and the matter continued to prey on his mind. Might Von Luck's men be watching him even now as he breakfasted? Would they shadow his every step? If so, how the devil was he to make contact with Meyer-Hoffman without putting the scientist in harm's way? For that matter, had the lack of a note from the doctor not been the result of the scientist wishing to exercise caution, but of his already being in the hands of the German agents? No, the latter could not possibly be the case because Von Luck's men would most certainly now have made for their escape across the Channel if they did already have hold of Meyer-Hoffman.

He fiddled with his teacup, bringing it to his lips then returning it to the saucer without taking a drink. What would Iain Moreland do in such a perplexing situation? One thing was for certain, Moreland would keep a calm head and a steady nerve. This was no time for fluster and worry.

Taking a deep breath and making a great effort to clear his mind, Templeman considered the matter in as calm and rational a manner as he could, rather as he might decide what clothes to wear for the day ahead based on the anticipated vagaries of the weather. What, he asked himself, was certain, what was mere speculation and what should his next steps be?

It was certainly the case that his room had been searched. It was also a reasonable assumption to make that he was now been watched by German agents. It seemed likewise to be an acceptable assumption that Meyer-Hoffman was not yet in the hands of Von Luck's men.

If all three of these considerations held true, then what would be his next and best course of action, bearing in mind that his primary objective was the safety of the German scientist? As he considered his options, the waiter returned with an offer of fresh tea.

"A splendid view you have here," commented Templeman.

"It is that," replied the waiter, a short, chunky man with some of the bushiest eyebrows Templeman could recall having seen. He reminded Templeman of the gruff, pipe-smoking gardener his parents had employed in his childhood. "A fine day's weather lies ahead, I'm told. Should be good walking conditions, if that's the sort of thing you're set on while you're with us, sir."

"I would, indeed, like to explore some of the countryside hereabouts," replied Templeman. "And you're absolutely right, it is fine walking weather."

As the waiter departed, Templeman relaxed back into his chair with a smile on his face. The waiter had solved his conundrum without even being aware he had done so. Solutions to even the trickiest of problems could come from the most unexpected of places.

With his reference to the weather being fine and good for walking, the waiter had pointed Templeman towards his next course of action. In matter of fact, it could almost be said that it was to be inaction. Instead of attempting to move matters along while he had no way of knowing how best to do so, Templeman decided he would show patience. Instead of going to the mountain, he would let the mountain come to him. Yes, he would let matters start to resolve themselves then make his move when it was right to do so.

Meyer-Hoffman had a start on him and was very likely right to exercise caution. A message would arrive soon enough, once the doctor determined it safe enough to deliver one. Then a meeting would be arranged. How they managed that without showing their hand to the German agents was something to be determined when the time came. Meyer-Hoffman was a clever and inventive man and may well have already worked out a solution to that particular problem.

In the meantime, Templeman intended to do just as the waiter had suggested and spend the morning enjoying a little exercise by taking a walk in the countryside. Perhaps he might even take the advice of his companions from the Red Lion and make a day of it by heading for Tenterden, which he had seen from his map lay several miles to the north-east. In fact, that was precisely what he would do. It would take his mind off other matters and leave plenty of time for things to develop of their own accord.

He strolled out of the dining room in a better mood by far than when he arrived, eager now to set off on his day's walk. However, he had not made it half-way to the stairs when the chap behind the reception desk called out to him.

"Mr Templeman. A message for you, sir. Hand-delivered just now."

How ironic, contemplated the agent, that at just the moment he had decided to stop worrying and allow matters to resolve themselves he should receive a message.

He took the slim white envelope from the receptionist and ran a thumb over the surface. It seemed a single sheet of paper lay inside.

"Did you see who delivered it?" he asked.

"A young boy. Not one I recognised, I'm afraid," replied the receptionist.

"Thank you," said Templeman, turning towards the stairs.

However, he was too impatient to know its contents to wait until reaching his room, so walked across to one of the big bay windows where he could be alone and tore open the envelope.

It was the news he had been hoping for. A message from Meyer-Hoffman. The scientist confirmed he was already in the town, though he neglected to say where he was staying, and was most anxious to meet Templeman. The proposed time and place for their rendezvous was noon that day, at the small wharf used by the fishing fleet, where a fish market operated most mornings.

Templeman felt a sense of relief at this contact from the scientist and was pleased they were to meet soon. He would have preferred to know where Meyer-Hoffman was staying but had to acknowledge that it was probably a wise caution for the scientist not to have included such information in the note. There was always the chance the note might get intercepted. Templeman pushed the concern aside, returned the sheet of notepaper to the envelope and dropped that into a jacket pocket.

As he took to the stairs, Templeman's thoughts returned to considering what to do next once he had met with Meyer-Hoffman. Ought he to insist on the scientist joining him at the hotel, so he would be close at hand should Von Luck's men make a move? Or perhaps the scientist had found more secure lodgings, where he should join him. And what about an escape route, should one prove necessary? It would allow them to move quickly if they knew where they were heading and how best to get there.

There were so many things to consider and Templeman felt a fool for not having thought of such matters sooner. However, at least he was now on the cusp of finding himself in a position to do what he had been sent there to do; his very best to ensure the doctor's safety. He wasn't a one-man army but, for now, at least, he was all there was.

THE FISH MARKET

To reach the wharf and fish market, Templeman left the town via the ancient Land Gate and followed a short stretch of road downhill, then round to the right until he reached lower ground at the base of the escapement, now on his right. Here he followed the road to the left, which led him up to the area's sole bridge over the River Rother.

Stopping here, as if he might be surveying the eddying, light brown waters of the river as it began to fall away from that morning's high tide, he checked to see if anyone might be following him. Now, of all times, he must ensure he exercised the greatest caution possible. One careless slip or lazy assumption and they might find themselves in the gravest of difficulties. But the road was empty of people, save for a small buggy pulled by a light brown mare that was trotting along the road north, towards the villages that lay outside of the town walls.

He had spent the best part of the previous hour pacing his room and checking his watch every few minutes, weighing up the competing merits and possible hazards of arriving at the rendezvous point more than a little early. On the one hand, it would provide him with time to assess the situation and ensure they were not under observation. On the other, such activity might of itself draw attention and that was one thing he did not wish to do. If Meyer-Hoffman had selected the location well, they would be meeting somewhere they could fully expect to be alone.

In the end, Templeman had compromised, not wanting to arrive excessively early but unable to restrain himself fully. As he turned on to the dirt track that led down to the riverside embankment, he could hear the church clock high up on the hill above him strike for a quarter to twelve.

The fishing fleet was tied up against the wharf, the half-dozen small boats bobbing casually in the swell, their masts tipping backwards and forwards as if in some orchestrated dance. Ropes lay neatly coiled on their decks, as saltwater-stained timbers glistened in the late morning sun. The smell of the sea and the river was strong, but it was overwhelmed by that of fish, of which there was, in matter of fact, precious little sign. There remained only the occasional scattering of scales and scraps that had not yet been found by the dozens of gulls that filled the sky, landing here and there to fight noisily over some small trophy.

Templeman saw but one solitary fisherman, a squat, heavy-set man whose eyes remained hidden under a wide-brimmed hat as he finished laying out a net to dry on a large wooden frame. He seemed not to notice Templeman and the agent slipped quietly past on his way towards the market and his rendezvous.

The market was a small wooden-framed building set under a tiled roof that had seen better days, there being numerous tiles either missing entirely or broken in parts. Three sides of the building were fully open to the weather, while on the fourth was a narrow, brick-built office with a single door facing the centre of the building. The main space was partially occupied by trellis tables, now empty but no doubt used for the display of the day's catch when the market was open.

Templeman took a turn around the whole of the building to ensure they would be alone and was content to find there were no other people to be found. As he took up station next to the welcome cover of the office, another look at his pocketwatch told him it was now ten minutes to twelve. He felt his heartbeat quicken. It would not be long now, but he felt certain those remaining ten minutes were going to be amongst some of the very slowest of his life.

However, half and hour late, he found himself checking his watch for the umpteenth time, having once again stepped out from under the cover of the fish market building to check in all directions for Meyer-Hoffman. Of the German scientist, there was still no sign. Indeed, there was no one whatsoever to be seen.

Templeman kicked at the stump of a rotting wooden post and rubbed a hand across the back of his neck. His brow had become so furrowed that he feared it must resemble a ploughed field and he was aware little drops of perspiration had formed at his temples, despite the coldness in the air.

It was so far beyond the time of their rendezvous that there was very little possibility of Meyer-Hoffman simply having been delayed. It was clear there was to be no meeting and what was now preying on Templeman's mind was the potential reason behind this. Had the doctor fallen ill or been involved in some unfortunate accident? It was a possibility. However, so was the notion that he had fallen into the hands of Von Luck's men. Perhaps they had been watching him since their arrival in the town or maybe he had been snatched on his way to the fish market.

Grim though the prospect was of Meyer-Hoffman now being a prisoner, it was the uncertainty that ate away at Templeman's nerves the most. If he only knew the nature of things, he could act accordingly. Instead, there he was, looking out at the now rapidly running river, as it rushed towards the sea, with no real intelligence on which to base his next move. It was a most unsettling situation.

He picked up a large, irregularly-shaped stone and hurled it out into the murky brown waters, where it was swallowed up with impunity.

Cursing his misfortune, Templeman took one last look at the fishing boats, now beginning to strain on their ropes as the river pushed by. As he did so, a thought came to him and he felt instantly relieved that he had taken the trouble to explore the town the previous day. It was the little, narrow wharf on the other side of town that came to mind. Had he not already told himself that it was the ideal place from which the German agents could make their escape into the Channel, should they get their hands on Meyer-Hoffman?

With a renewed sense of purpose and urgency, Templeman strode away towards the Land Gate, hoping above all else that he was not already too late. If a small boat was to head for the sea, it would need to do so now, on the falling tide, or else wait until tomorrow. As he approached the river bridge, he broke into a trot.

*

It was twenty minutes to two when Templeman sloped back into the entrance hall of the Queen Charlotte, his shoulders drooping and his features long and drawn. His hopes of finding Meyer-Hoffman at the wharf, even should he be in the hands of several devious German agents, had come to nothing. Enquiries about the possible appearance of German subjects at the wharf had drawn no positive replies. Either his notion had been a false one or he'd been too late and the doctor was at this very moment being bundled aboard a yacht that lay at anchor in the Channel.

The unhappy agent had begun to wonder how on earth he was going to break such disheartening news to Sir Joshua when he was snapped out of his funk by a call from the receptionist.

"Mr Templeman. A message for you, sir."

UNCERTAINTIES ABOUND

Templeman's spirits lifted at once. Could it be Meyer-Hoffman, contacting him to explain his absence and suggesting another rendezvous? He took possession of the new envelope eagerly.

"Thank you," he said to the receptionist as he slit it open.

Templeman's initial reaction on seeing the single sheet of white paper inside was one of confusion. It was a telegram, not a hand-written note. What could this mean? He pulled out the sheet of paper and unfolded it. Surely it could not be from Meyer-Hoffman? His eyes moved to the bottom of the paper and there he saw that it was signed JC. Sir Joshua.

The concerned agent quickly scanned the short message. As expected, Templeman found that the message from Sir Joshua was written in code, a seemingly mundane paragraph, asking him to keep a look out for naval paintings during his stay in the town. The real meaning of the note would need to be decoded.

Templeman hastened back to his room, where it took him twenty minutes of steady, laborious labour to extract the hidden message, using the text of the Wilkie Collins novel The Moonstone, which was currently the Bureau's reference work for encoding and decoding their messages. In truth, it was a rather simple arrangement, but a most practical one where more complex alternatives were not available.

The message was brief and not altogether helpful, though that was through no fault of Sir Joshua's.

T, be aware, there is reason to believe Von Luck now has agents in Rye. No progress made with the in-house issue. Exercise great caution.

JC.

The lack of progress in identifying the traitor at the Bureau was not unexpected and the news about Von Luck's men was disappointing, even if it did confirm his earlier suspicions. Templeman had hoped the telegram might have delivered better news and the lack of this served only to darken his mood further.

Setting light to both the original message and the decoded version, Templeman dropped the two pieces of paper into the fireplace and watched them turn to dust before turning his mind back to the issue of Meyer-Hoffman.

It seemed he had two choices. He could assume the worst and consider Meyer-Hoffman to now be in the hands of Von Luck's men, in all likelihood already a prisoner on a yacht making its way up the English Channel towards the north German coast. Although an unwelcome prospect it did seem to have a good deal going for it. The German agents were most definitely active in the town, the scientist had supposedly escaped cover in order to meet him at the fish market and the tides had been in the German agents' favour.

However, there was also the possibility that something else entirely had occurred. That, for whatever currently unknown reason, Meyer-Hoffman had either not been able to make their rendezvous or had seen it as necessary not to show up. The problem with this possibility was the lack of any further message from the scientist. Surely the doctor would have taken the trouble to let him know that he remained safely ensconced in his hideaway?

As Templeman stood by the window, watching the world

pass by, he came to the conclusion that, even if Meyer-Hoffman was now once more in German hands, until this became a known reality he should operate on the basis that hope remained. There was little doubt that the wrong thing to do was to assume the worst and remain idly there doing nothing at all.

Quite what he could do remained the greatest of frustrations for Templeman. Opportunities for action seemed limited in the extreme, given his almost total ignorance of the situation. But, finally, a thought occurred to him. In such a small town, it must surely be the case that somebody, somewhere would be aware of the presence of German visitors. Even if the German agents spoke faultless English, he doubted it would be entirely free of an accent and he knew, for a fact, that Meyer-Hoffman spoke with a pronounced German accent.

With that being the case, Templeman decided to recommence his efforts at tracking down either the scientist or Von Luck's men. He would begin by calling at every hotel in the town, then, if he'd had no success at that point, he would move on to lodging houses. People needed somewhere to rest their head at night and, even if they kept their conversation to a minimum, they would still need to speak to hotel staff or the owners of lodging houses.

His task might take him all day to complete, but, as Templeman snatched up his coat, he did so with a renewed sense of vigour and purpose. What might occur should he find Von Luck's men, he had no idea. But that was a matter to be dealt with if the situation arose. For now his focus was on finding them and thereby putting the initiative in his own hands for what would be the first time since he had arrived in Rye.

But as he reached for the door handle to let himself out into the hallway, Templeman stopped and gave a little shake of the head.

"Careful, my good fellow. Careful." he said to himself, taking a step back.

It had occurred to him that, if he was to take the initiative, somehow or other he had to throw off the agent he had good reason to believe would be waiting for him outside the hotel, no doubt hidden from view. It would give him no advantage if he allowed himself to be followed all over town. Indeed, it was most likely that the German agent would soon realise what he was up to and make haste to warn his fellows.

But how was he to throw off his adversary? He needed some means of doing so without arousing suspicion. Then it came to Templeman that, while lounging around in the reception area, he had seen a member of staff enter a room at the rear of the building then re-appear dressed in their hotel uniform. A change of clothes might do the job, he considered. Perhaps even a disguise of some sort. Yes, that would do very nicely indeed.

Making his way downstairs, Templeman let himself into the changing room without any issue and was pleased to find several sets of men's clothes hanging on pegs. Finding one that looked a good match for his size, he slipped out of his own clothes and put on the stranger's garments. There was a well-worn, somewhat smelly cap as well, so he took that and pulled it down over his eyes. After briefly practising a less measured and gentlemanly way of walking, he let himself out of the room and then the side entrance to the hotel. Turning left, this brought him out on to the street a short distance on from the hotel's main entrance.

His hand found a packet of cigarettes and a box of matches in one of the pockets of the heavy woollen coat. Keeping his face shielded by the peak of the cap, he placed a cigarette in his mouth and lit it. As he drew on the cigarette for the first time, he glanced casually up and down the street. Men and women of all classes walked by, some hurrying others dawdling. An elderly woman, perhaps some sort of nurse, pushed a large blue pram which she rocked gently as she did so. On the far side of the road a scruffy child, no more than three or four years of age, skipped along the top of the low-set brick wall that skirted the street.

But there, leaning against a more substantial length of stone wall down towards the Land Gate, was a tall, broad-shouldered man with dark hair, wrapped in a long grey woollen coat. Templeman might have thought nothing of him if not for the fact the man's attention seemed entirely taken by the Queen Charlotte, which he observed without a break. There was no one else to be seen that Templeman thought a likely suspect, so he determined this was the man he needed to throw off his track.

Stepping out on to the street, Templeman began to walk towards the town centre, reminding himself to move as any working man would, not like a gentleman. He was, he told himself, a man who'd just finished a shift of work and was now on his way home to a welcoming wife and two or three bright-eyed children.

Although he had seen no movement from the suspected German agent, Templeman thought it wise to exercise caution. Seeing a narrow alley that led off the High Street down the steep slope, he turned into it and skipped down the steps until he reached a small open area to his right. Here he leaned back against the red brick wall of a house and began to smoke as if reluctant to return home.

By the time he had finished the cigarette there had been no sign of anyone else using the alleyway. Confident he had fooled his adversary, Templeman navigated the remaining steps, then turned to his left, having determined he would begin his search at the southern end of the town.

*

It was a quarter-past six when Templeman returned to his room at the Queen Charlotte, his feet sore and his lips parched. He was back in his own clothes and the owner of his disguise seemed not to have noticed his clothes had been missing. Templeman had also seen there was now a different man leaning against the wall down by the Land Gate and it left him in no doubt whatsoever that he was being watched and that was the spot the enemy had selected for their observation post.

If that was a positive addition to his store of intelligence, then less helpful had been the outcome of his afternoon's labours, for he had enjoyed no success in trying to track down any Germans that were staying in the town. Indeed, given his appearance, it had proved impossible to extract an answer from staff at two of the larger hotels, who had kicked him out almost as soon as he had made his enquiry.

He had already decided that, should there be no other developments, he would continue his search the following morning. The simple act of being engaged in such a pursuit had relieved him of the anxiety he had been experiencing earlier, which was a most welcome development in itself.

It had also occurred to him that the very presence of the German agents seemed to suggest they had not found Meyer-Hoffman. Surely had they done so they would have quickly left the town? That thought alone encouraged him to continue his search.

Both Meyer-Hoffman and Von Luck's men had to be staying somewhere in the town and it must surely be only a matter of time and persistence until he located them. The thought briefly flickered through his mind that perhaps the German agents might be hiding out on the marsh, but that appeared such a desolate place it would hardly be likely to offer anywhere suitable. There was also the option of turning the tables on his enemies and attempting to follow one of the agents when they were relieved at the end of their shift.

But all that was for tomorrow. Having washed and changed, Templeman made his way downstairs for dinner, famished as a result of so much exercise. He would select the largest possible meal from the menu this evening, whatever that might turn out to be.

As he stepped off the bottom step, a now familiar voice hailed him from the reception desk.

"Another message for you, sir."

Extraordinary, thought Templeman. There he had been,

waiting anxiously for but a single message from Meyer-Hoffman and now, barely a day later, messages were arriving in droves. Who could it be this time? Sir Joshua with further news, perhaps? Maybe there had now been some sort of development with unmasking the traitor. That would be welcome indeed. He took the envelope and walked through to the dining room, where he secured a table by a window. Then, having ordered a gin and tonic, he opened this latest correspondence. His eyes lit up when he saw that it was, in fact, from Meyer-Hoffman.

The Sultan of Zanzire

A CALL FOR HELP

The note was handwritten, in near-perfect English, though its somewhat florid nature meant Templeman had to proceed more slowly than he normally would. In it, Meyer-Hoffman went to some lengths to explain his failure to make their rendezvous and the perceived nature of his current situation.

Dear Sir,

Please allow me to begin by offering my sincerest apologies for my failure to meet you at the fish market today as I had previously requested. As I endeavour to explain in this brief letter my situation has become rather precarious and I found it necessary to alter my arrangements at somewhat short notice.

I had hoped that, in choosing to remove myself to Rye, after the attempted abduction by Von Luck's men at Waterloo railway terminus, I would be somewhere safe until such time as Sir Joshua could make arrangements for me to be escorted to whatever place he deemed appropriate for the longer term. I should add that Rye is a pretty little town that my wife and I have visited on two previous occasions, so I already had some familiarity with the place, which I expected would be helpful to me.

All went as hoped at first. I found a quiet, modest hotel that provided me with all the amenities I needed without any need to leave the premises and I telegrammed Sir Joshua, so as to inform him of my situation. He replied promptly to say that you, and you alone, would be travelling down to Rye to meet me and that he expected we would remain in the town for a further few days. He also noted the hotel you would be staying at.

Thus, I was able to send you a note asking to meet me at the fish market, where I anticipated we could agree on how best to see out the time until we heard once more from Sir Joshua.

However, matters began to take a concerning turn yesterday evening. When I returned from dinner I found that my room had been searched. Some people, no doubt, would have thought they were imagining such a thing had happened, but you must understand that I am a most particular individual. It is necessary to be so for my work. It was, therefore, easy for me to see that someone had been through all my belongings.

I could not, for one minute, imagine how Von Luck must have been able to establish that I was now in Rye, but such a consideration was immaterial; it seemed excessively unlikely that anyone else would have been through my belongings, since, if it had been a thief then they would have stolen my more valuable items and this was not so.

Still hesitating, somewhat, I decided to proceed with our arrangement thinking that you would know best what to do next. However, upon making my way down the stairs on the way to meet you, I overheard a conversation between my landlady and a man who had his back towards me. His accent was unmistakably German. There could be no doubt about the changed nature of my situation. I had been tracked down by Von Luck's agents and to remain where I was meant certain capture.

Without any delay, I returned to my room, packed up my few belongings and found a back way out of the building. It was then but a brief affair to find for myself some new lodgings elsewhere in the town. I believe that I remain safe for the time being, but this state of affairs cannot be expected to continue for long. I ask, therefore, that you meet me at noon tomorrow at the Ypres Tower and come ready for the two of us to escape the town at once. I am sure that with your training and skills we ought to be able to do so unobserved by our pursuers and find for ourselves some other town where we can go into hiding.

I suggest the Ypres Tower, I might add, because I believe that I can for now get there unobserved and because I do not believe Von Luck's men would risk a second public attempt to snatch me after the abject failure of their previous effort. Let us, nonetheless, hope that we do not set eyes on these odious individuals.

I do hope this brief note clarifies why I was unable to make our earlier meeting, the most hazardous situation I am now in and our urgent need to flee the town.

I much look forward to our meeting once again.

Most sincerely yours,
Dr P. Meyer-Hoffman

Whilst Templeman couldn't help observing that the note was hardly as brief as Meyer-Hoffman seemed to believe, it had at least provided him with a solid understanding of the doctor's current situation and their joint need to take urgent action.

Meyer-Hoffman was right to conclude that they ought to move on elsewhere and be prompt about it. But the first question this posed was where to move to? The second was how to do so unobserved by Von Luck's men. The first ought to be answered without a great deal of effort, but the second was an entirely different matter. It was likely to prove quite the challenge.

Templeman felt an odd mingling of both relief and excitement at receiving this letter. Relief that the scientist remained at liberty, excitement, tinged with a little apprehension, at the prospect of action. But action had been what he'd longed for these past two days and now his wish had come true.

He re-read the doctor's letter before tucking it into a jacket pocket. He would destroy the correspondence once he returned to his room; it was best not to take any chances with such things. He then called over the waiter. If action it was to be, then he should take care to eat a hearty meal, for he was going to need all the energy he could muster the following day.

By the time he had polished off his food and was swirling a somewhat questionable brandy in its glass, Templeman had decided what enquiries he would need to make the following morning in order to identify another town that might suit their needs. He had also begun to formulate a number of different options that might facilitate their safe and unobserved flight from Rye. It was the latter challenge that continued to concern him, however, since it was essential they throw off their pursuers. Prior experience of such things told him, all too plainly, that was something more easily said than done.

As he climbed into a chilly bed later that evening, Templeman had devised several alternatives for their flight, none of which were entirely satisfactory but nonetheless held out hope of success. He was still running through them in his mind, looking for possible hazards and ways to address these, when he eventually drifted off into what was to be a fitful nights sleep.

RENDEZVOUS

The following morning, after a breakfast of eggs and bacon, which he consumed hurriedly, Templeman made his way to reception, where he made enquiries as to the surrounding towns, seeking to get an idea of their nature and the available transport links. Several options presented themselves, most notably Hastings to the west, Royal Tunbridge Wells to the north and Dover to the east. All three seemed to be suitably sized as to offer plenty of opportunity for him and Meyer-Hoffman to lose themselves amongst the crowd, as it were, and all three had transport links to London, which he considered important.

His initial task of the morning completed, Templeman returned to his room where he packed his bags in readiness for an anticipated departure. He then slipped unobserved out of the back entrance to the hotel once more and set off to call at a number of establishments in the town. These calls would put in train three different sets of preparations for fleeing the town later that day. By so doing, Templeman aimed to give himself and the scientist other options should the German agents become aware of or block their flight to his preferred destination of Royal Tunbridge Wells, a place of which he had some little knowledge, having visited with his parents as a child.

His various enquiries, more than one of which necessitated making additional calls at further establishments, took up the greater part of the morning and, by the time they were complete, his feet ached and he was growing desperate for a refreshing drink. As he heard the church clock strike eleven, Templeman entered at a little tea shop on The Mint, towards the southern end of town, where he ordered scones and a pot of tea.

Unfolding the copy of The Times he had purchased earlier, he sat back and did his best to relax, having decided that upon leaving the tea shop he would head straight up the hill to the Ypres Tower and his rendezvous with Meyer-Hoffman. There was no need to return to the Queen Charlotte for now. All the necessary arrangements were made and all that remained was to meet the doctor, ensure he was in good health, then inform him of their escape route. After that, they could leave. Hopefully without being pursued.

*

Templeman turned off the High Street and on to Lion Street, heading up the short, steep hill towards St Mary's Church, which he needed to skirt round as he made his way to the Ypres Tower. He had calculated his time of departure from the tea shop rather carefully, anxious not to risk being seen by Von Luck's men should he loiter within the environs of the Tower. He would get there only a minute or two before noon.

However, as he was about to pass a premises dealing in antiquarian books, Templeman's eye was caught by an animated figure nearby on the pavement. It was an elderly woman with a stern face, wearing a hat of such size it was a wonder the wind hadn't swept her away.

She called out to him, "You there, I am in need of your assistance."

Templeman pretended he had not noticed the woman and made to stride on past.

"Young man. Young man. I will have your attention," the woman demanded in a voice that sounded all too like that of a nursery nurse or a hospital matron.

Templeman found his way was now blocked by an outstretched umbrella. He stopped, took a deep breath and turned to face this wholly unwelcome obstruction. This was going to take time he could not spare.

"How can I help you, madam?"

"I'm trying to find Mermaid Street and for the life of me I can't work it out. I do believe I've been going round in circles. You must point me in the right direction," she commanded, her small eyes boring into Templeman in a manner that made him feel distinctly unsettled.

"I would be only too happy to assist, but I'm not a native of these parts and, unfortunately, have not the slightest idea where to find Mermaid Street." He was aware that he couldn't altogether stop the irritation he felt from showing in his voice.

The woman's eyes narrowed. "Then perhaps you'd like to find a policeman. He'll be able to show me the way. I'm sure even an impatient young man like you can locate a policeman."

Templeman was about to risk causing considerable offence by brushing aside the umbrella, when, quite remarkably, he saw a constable round the corner at the bottom of the road and start walking towards them. He smiled.

"Indeed, I can, madam." He waved a hand to catch the attention of the officer, who promptly quickened his step.

"Good afternoon, sir. Madam," said the constable. "How can I be of assistance?"

"Constable, this lady…"

"Never mind. Never mind. Off you go, you rude man. Everyone in such a hurry," added the aggrieved woman as she jabbed Templeman with her umbrella before he could escape her reach.

As he rushed on up the hill and by St Mary's Church, Templeman heard the bells begin to chime for noon. He was now late. He began to run at a trot, careless of the attention it drew from passers-by. The doctor, he knew, would be on time; that is, assuming nothing had happened to put an end to this attempt at their meeting.

As it was, as Templeman approached the Tower, with the Methodist church to his right, he feared the delay caused by the persistent old woman might have proved fatal to his plans. There ahead of him, closing on the entrance to the Tower, was a tall, broad-shouldered man who looked for certain to be one of the pair he had seen keeping the Queen Charlotte under close observation.

Templeman stopped involuntarily and felt his already quickened heart rate ratchet up a notch. If the doctor had already arrived and was even now waiting somewhere inside the Tower, it seemed certain this agent of the enemy was going to reach him first. Then, at the very moment Templeman went to take another step forward, the tall man turned and called out to a young boy who was dilly-dallying some yards further down the road, playing with a stick that he scraped repeatedly against the brick wall of a house.

Templeman could see the man's face now, as he beckoned the boy to hurry up, and it was clear it wasn't the same man he had seen waiting down by the Land Gate. As a welcome sense of relief swept over him, Templeman let out a deep breath before closing out the remaining twenty yards to the Tower entrance.

As he stepped into the cool, gloomy confines of the Tower, Templeman began to wonder where the doctor might be waiting for him. Meyer-Hoffman had neglected to be specific about such things in his rather lengthy letter and there was quite a notable amount of ground to cover. However, it seemed the scientist had thought of this himself, for Templeman had taken only a few steps when Meyer-Hoffman appeared from behind a section of stone wall.

"Templeman. A little late but I am most pleased to see you," said the German, holding out a hand in greeting.

"Ah, there you are, doctor," replied the agent, temporarily caught off balance. "Excellent." He shook the scientist's hand. "And you have your luggage I see."

"Yes, I am well prepared."

Meyer-Hoffman was holding the same suitcase he had arrived with at Portsmouth, but Templeman quickly noticed that he no longer seemed to have possession of his briefcase.

"Your briefcase, Doctor? Do you still have it?"

The scientist looked around him then took hold of Templeman's shoulder and began to steer him towards a corner of the room.

"If you please. We cannot be too careful."

"Yes, of course. I quite understand."

Standing now between two somewhat tatty suits of Medieval armour mounted on display stands, the two men huddled together and when he next spoke, Meyer-Hoffman did so quietly.

"You are certain you were not followed?" he asked.

"Absolutely," replied Templeman. "I've spent the morning going about our business all over the town and I can confidently state that had there been someone following me I would have spotted them long ago. And yourself, Doctor, are you confident Von Luck's men have not picked up your tracks again?"

"I believe not. I have been here for thirty minutes, most observant the whole time, and have seen no one who drew my suspicions."

"Good. Very good. So we are safe, for now," said Templeman. "But your briefcase. Has it been lost?"

Meyer-Hoffman shook his head.

"No, it is not lost, but it was no longer of any purpose. You see, after the events at Waterloo railway terminus, once I had recovered my senses having escaped that terrible scene, I took some time to consider my position. I came to the conclusion that it would be the correct thing to do to separate me from my papers. In that case, should the worst come to happen and I fall back into the hands of Von Luck's men then the British Government will still have access to my papers. That should be sufficient to allow their own scientists to progress my work."

"Outstanding thinking, doctor," said Templeman, relieved to hear that the papers had not been lost. "So, what have you done with these papers?"

"I made use of a security deposit box at a London bank. There I put my papers in store and then gave my briefcase to a desperate looking, how you say, urchin, on the street. I have the key to the deposit box here," he added, patting a pocket on his jacket.

A burst of noise from the entrance interrupted their conversation and they remained silent as they waited for a small group of visitors to pass on through. A young girl stopped, looked up at Meyer-Hoffman for a moment, then stuck her tongue out before running off to catch up with the rest of her party.

"Ah, the young children, they are very amusing, are they not?" smiled the scientist, as he watched the girl disappear from view.

"Er, indeed," replied Templeman. "Very amusing."

Meyer-Hoffman gave a chuckle before bringing his attention back to the English agent.

"Have you a plan for our escape?" asked the scientist.

"I have, indeed," answered Templeman. "My activities across town this morning were concerned with making three separate sets of arrangements for our flight to another town. All of them are now in place, so that we have alternatives immediately at hand should my preferred option of moving on to Tunbridge Wells be blocked."

"But you have no luggage?" enquired the German.

"Indeed, not. Now that we have made contact I will slip back to my hotel, collect my bags then return here. I would have preferred we depart by train, but there is too much likelihood that Von Luck's men will have the railway station under observation. Instead, we will take a bus from the town's depot that will carry us all the way to Tunbridge Wells. It will be a slow and no doubt uncomfortable journey, but is, I trust, by far the safer option."

"We go now?" asked the eager-sounding scientist.

"Indeed, we do. Just as soon as I collect my luggage. I managed to locate a back entrance to the hotel, which I've been using these past two days, since I established I have been under observation, quite possibly since the moment I arrived."

"That is a matter that has been perplexing me most disagreeably," commented Meyer-Hoffman. "How is it that Von Luck knew where to send his men? I had thought such a small and out of the way place as this would not attract their attention for even a moment. It is very concerning."

Templeman was anxious not to worry the scientist further by sharing Sir Joshua's belief that Von Luck has secured a traitor within the Bureau. "Yes, but, there it is; they somehow or other managed to track us down and now we must do our best to escape them. Once we reach Tunbridge Wells, I plan on contacting Sir Joshua to ask for reinforcements. It's hard to think our pursuers won't eventually track us down there and we would be wise to be ready for them."

"Quite so," said Meyer-Hoffman. "I wish only that I am once more in the warm embrace of my wonderful Helen. A man has truly never had a more loving wife. And she is so strong of heart. More so than I am myself. It has been so very hard these last few days being without her company."

"Fear not, doctor, we'll get you to her just as soon as it's safe to do so."

"I hope it is soon," replied Meyer-Hoffman, sounding for all the world as if he feared he might never see his beloved wife again. "Ah, but I nearly forget myself," he said, once again alive with energy. "How is Herr Moreland? I saw that he was shot, but I am afraid I was not there long enough to see how he fared. I hope that he is making a good recovery?"

"He is, indeed. Poor fellow would dearly have loved to be

here now, but it will be some little while until he is sufficiently recovered to be back on active service." Templeman pulled out his pocketwatch. "But we must make haste. The bus we are to catch departs at one-fifteen. Keep yourself to the shadows here and as soon as I return we will make our way across town to the bus depot. Let's hope we are not spotted on the way."

With that, Templeman left the scientist to await his return, wishing they were already on the bus and with the town of Rye far behind them. The hour that remained before their departure was sure to be one of the most fraught of his life and their chances of success were perhaps no more than fifty-fifty.

He was, in fact, still weighing up the possibilities some twenty minutes later, as he approached the Tower for the second time that morning, now with his luggage in hand. He had just reached the Methodist Church, when a horrified shout of alarm went up from amid a small group of sightseers milling about the Tower entrance. A hand was jabbed skywards. Templeman stopped and followed the line of the outstretched arm up towards the ramparts of the Tower.

Templeman froze. There, pressed hard up against the very edge of the building was the figure of Meyer-Hoffman. He was struggling with another man, a large imposing figure who seemed to have a solid grip on him. For a moment it looked as if the bigger man might be attempting to push the doctor over the edge, but then he appeared to drag the scientist away, out of sight of those below.

The little party of sightseers were all now excitedly and noisily staring upwards, pointing at the ramparts, but Templeman had quickly come to his senses. Dropping his small suitcase, he ran the last few yards to the Tower and plunged through the entrance, his heart beating frantically.

A DESPERATE ENCOUNTER

The stone stairs that led from one level of the Tower to the next were narrow and the individual steps higher than normal, which made navigating them an awkward and tiring exercise. As he reached the second floor of the building, Templeman was already breathing heavily and his legs were beginning to ache.

He was about to head on up the final flight when he heard raised voices coming from an open doorway on the far side of a huge room he was standing on the edge of. Feet appeared on the steps he could see through the doorway and he had a fancy the shoes were the doctor's. It seemed he was being escorted down off the ramparts.

Moving quickly, Templeman ducked behind the cover of a thick stone column that supported the roof, then, believing himself to be out of sight, stepped across the wooden floor to the next column. He slipped a hand inside a coat pocket and let his fingers caress the gun he had placed there before leaving the hotel. A gun battle would be his final, desperate option, since it would risk injury or even death to the scientist, but if fired upon by Von Luck's men he was fully prepared to return that fire.

Leaning with care around the side of the pillar, he saw

Meyer-Hoffman pushed roughly into the room by the tall, broad-shouldered German agent he'd seen before. Behind him came a shorter, though no less well-built, accomplice. He had expected his next move would be to follow the three men down the staircase they were already using, but for some reason they left that one behind and entered the room, heading towards the staircase Templeman had just navigated.

The Englishman felt somewhat how he imagined a lion or a leopard might feel as they stalked game on the African savannah. His prey remained oblivious to his presence, allowing him to manoeuvre to his advantage as he waited for them to close the gap on him. Two to one. The odds were, he thought, not at all bad, given he had the element of surprise on his side. The only significant concern was Meyer-Hoffman. One false move, a single miscalculation and Templeman might find himself responsible for the scientist's death.

But there was nothing for it. He had to act and the time for that was now. Pulling air slowly and deeply into this lungs, then releasing it just as carefully, Templeman felt his heart rate begin to slow a little. He wiped the sweat from the palm of his right hand, then pulled the gun from out of his pocket.

But, just as he set himself to act there was a stroke of good fortune. Meyer-Hoffman was first to pass the column behind which Templeman was hiding and the scientist caught sight of him out of the corner of his eye. With admirable presence of mind, the doctor sought to take advantage of this by stumbling and falling to his knees. As he clambered back to his feet his two captors stepped past him, spitting insults at his clumsiness.

Not wasting a second, Templeman leapt out behind the two German agents, his gun pointed towards them.

"Thank you, gentlemen," he said, in as calm a voice as he could manage. "I will take the doctor from here." One of the enemy agents moved a hand towards a coat pocket. "No," commanded Templeman. "Hands on your heads, if you please. Where I can see them." He glanced at the doctor, who was now back on his feet. "Head towards those stairs," he said to the scientist. "Best keep yourself out of the way until the police arrive. Someone will have sent for them by now."

As the doctor made towards the doorway, the two German agents, timing their movements together, dived for the nearest available cover, seemingly unconcerned that Templeman had a gun trained on them. Much to the British agent's frustration, it seemed they were right to consider their odds respectable, for the one shot he got off missed its intended target by a wide margin.

"Take cover, doctor," he yelled as he swung his gun around to take fresh aim at the larger man, who was scrambling behind the partial cover of a large oak table.

But it was the other enemy agent who got away a shot first, a deafening crack bouncing off the stone walls as a bullet smacked against the column which Templeman was now retreating behind. Another two shots quickly rang out from the taller man as he took aim over the top of the table.

Rolling round the side of the stone column, Templeman opened up a clear line of sight on the taller agent and promptly fired off two further shots of his own. The first bullet he was disappointed to see send up a shower of wooden splinters, but the second hit home, knocking the tall man backwards.

Immediately, a flurry of bullets crashed into the stone column above Templeman's head and he dived to the floor, the echo of the noise reverberating in his ears. Scrambling once more behind the column, he could hear movement from the enemy agents and he was about to swing round so he could take another shot when he stopped dead.

There, slumped on the ground leaning up against the stone archway, almost within reach of cover, was Meyer-Hoffman. He was holding a hand to his chest and a red liquid was running down the back of his fingers.

Templeman peered round the side of the column and

found the smaller of Von Luck's men helping his larger fellow into the cover of the other staircase. He saw one of them stop in the shadows then heard him call out in a harsh mocking voice, "We have what we came for, Templeman. We leave the dying traitor, Meyer-Hoffman, with you. He is of no use to us now."

Templeman fired a shot in the direction of the stairway, but it was now entirely empty. His adversaries were seeking to make their escape. He briefly considered going after them but knew his priority was to attend to the German scientist, so turned and hurried across the room.

Meyer-Hoffman's face was pale and the amount of blood that had soaked into his clothing looked to be considerable. Templeman eased open the doctor's coat and shirt to find he had been hit not once but twice, once in the shoulder, once in his chest.

The scientist looked up, coughed and blood trickled from the corner of his mouth.

"It is not good, eh, Templeman?" The German struggled to get the words out and began coughing again.

"Steady there, doctor. Best not to try talking. Here, let me rest your head on this," said Templeman as he pulled off his coat, rolled it up and propped it behind the scientist's neck. "Steady breaths. You hold on there while I have someone fetch a doctor. There must be one nearby."

Meyer-Hoffman managed to reach out a hand and took a weak grip on Templeman's arm.

"No, it is too late," the scientist said, his voice growing weak. "The key. They have the key…" he coughed again, more violently this time.

"It's nothing to worry about," replied Templeman. "They won't get far. We'll have them before they can make use of that key."

The doctor's eyes began to glaze over and Templeman could see the man was clearly struggling with all his might to say what he needed to.

"Lighthouse," whispered Meyer-Hoffman. "Lighthouse."

He was speaking so quietly now that Templeman could hardly hear what he said.

"A lighthouse. I understand. A lighthouse."

Meyer-Hoffman's hand slipped off Templeman's arm and on to the floor.

His eyes closed and, with a final soft sigh, he said the one word, "Helen," and then his head slipped to one side.

"Doctor," prodded Templeman with great concern. "Doctor Hoffman."

There was no reply. No words. No movement. Templeman leaned forward and put an ear close to the scientist's mouth. There was no indication the man was still breathing. Still hoping for the best, Templeman searched for a pulse, first on Meyer-Hoffman's wrist, then at his temple. But there was none to be found.

Templeman sat back against the wall, closed his eyes and let out a deep breath. Meyer-Hoffman was dead. His mission had been a failure. He had been unable to keep the scientist safe and secure, out of reach of Von Luck's ruthless butchers. He slammed a fist against the ground and uttered profanities of the sort he rarely found the need to use.

How on earth was he to explain matters to Sir Joshua? And the consequences for the country? Templeman's head tilted forward, his chin resting on his chest. He wasn't sure he could recall ever experiencing a greater sense of loss and of his own abject inadequacies. But some faint light of self-belief remained flickering inside him and it quickly pushed itself above the surface of his anguish. He had, after all, been faced with two determined adversaries, both of them armed. He, on the other hand, had not only himself to protect but also Meyer-Hoffman. Perhaps he was, after all, being a little too harsh on himself.

And then he recalled what the scientist had said as he lay dying. A lighthouse. Templeman's eyes flicked open and he tried to recall precisely what Meyer-Hoffman had said. But all he could remember the scientist saying was that one word, lighthouse. What the devil was he talking about? And what could it possibly have to do with anything that mattered?

As he struggled to see what a lighthouse might have to do with Meyer-Hoffman, Templeman recalled that he had, in fact, seen a lighthouse recently. But where, that was the question? He began to work through his recollections of the past two days, carefully analysing the places he had been and the sights he had seen.

And then it came to him. Oh, such irony. Some people, he contemplated, might call it fate, but he believed in no such thing. It was blind luck. Coincidence of the most heartless kind. It was on his first visit to the Tower that he had seen a lighthouse. Standing outside, looking out over the battlements, across the marsh, he had spotted, way off in the distance, the distinct tall, narrow shape of a lighthouse.

But what could it possibly have to do with Meyer-Hoffman? Or was he asking the wrong question? Yes, perhaps it wasn't the dead scientist he should be thinking about, but Von Luck's men. In which case, what use could they possibly have for a lighthouse? Templeman rubbed vigorously at his temples.

"Think man. Think," he barked at himself.

Of course. Perhaps they had never intended to escape out into the Channel from the little wharf in the town, with its unhelpful tides and public situation. It was only he who had thought that must be their way out. Perhaps he was, after all, entirely wrong about that. Maybe they were to be picked up from the shore by a small boat, in which case what better location was there for signalling your request to some waiting yacht out in the Channel than a lighthouse.

Maybe he could yet reach the fleeing German agents before they made good their escape. After all, he had winged one of them badly and that was sure to slow them down. Were there just the two of them or could there be more who had formed into some little band before taking flight for the lighthouse? It didn't matter. All that did was the thought he might still be able to retrieve the key to the security deposit box. Not only that, it might also present him with the chance to exact revenge for the murder of Meyer-Hoffman.

Templeman climbed to his feet and looked once more at the dead scientist. Such a waste of a brilliant mind and a fine man, not to mention the distress it would bring to his widow.

The sound of voices echoed up the stairwell on the far side of the room, snapping Templeman out of his thoughts. He reached down and picked up the gun he had left lying on the floor, slipping it into a jacket pocket, then collected up his coat.

As the voices grew louder, Templeman swiftly weighed up the respective merits and disadvantages of bringing the police in on his mission. The additional manpower was the chief benefit, plus a better knowledge and understanding of the local landscape than he possessed himself.

But the potential drawbacks were greater. For one thing, he would no doubt be required to explain, possibly at great length, the events of the past two days in Rye and those since Meyer-Hoffman's arrival at Portsmouth. Aside from any considerations of secrecy, this would take time, no doubt quite a lot of time, and that was something he did not have. No, it was imperative he act quickly if he was to have any chance of reaching the lighthouse before the German agents made good their escape.

Of course, that presupposed he was right about the lighthouse; both that he had the right one in mind and that he had correctly identified its purpose. But that was the best he could do and so now he needed to act swiftly. With one final glance at the dead scientist, Templeman stepped into the stairwell.

As he came out on to the windswept terrace at the rear of the Tower, he paused to look out to the east. There, so far away it was only just visible, he could make out the narrow upright that was the lighthouse. It might as well have been at the end of the world, it looked so remote. Templeman contemplated that, should things not go well for him, it would indeed be the end of his world.

THE EDGE OF THE WORLD

Templeman wasn't at all certain of the distance to the lighthouse, but he did know it wasn't a journey to be undertaken on foot. Having briefly considered and dismissed the possibility of getting there by boat, on the basis that his approach would be easily visible, he searched around for some other option.

He was in luck, promptly finding a man with a horse-drawn cart who was happy to carry him there for a modest fee, as he was already heading for one of the small coastal towns on the far side of the marsh. The carter informed him that the lighthouse was operated by a single keeper who lived there all year round, save for one week in the summer, when he travelled north to visit relatives, and two days at Christmas, which he spent with the same family. Templeman was warned that the lighthouse keeper was a craggy old fellow, who liked being on his own and rarely took kindly to visitors, particularly ones who were strangers to him.

The journey would, Templeman was informed, take around forty minutes, the distance being some two miles and the roads not being good. Forty minutes, he repeated to himself, when told this. That was longer than he had hoped for and he wondered what form of transport the German agents would be using and how long it would take them to reach the lighthouse. But there was nothing he could do about that, other than hope for the best.

Thus, as they navigated the Monk Bretton Bridge, the sole crossing point on that stretch of the Rother, Templeman settled down, huddled deep inside his coat, listening to the clip-clop of the horse's shoes on the road and watching the thickening clouds scudding across the sky. It was a hard business holding on to his patience and he could feel the tension tight within his body. He felt sure that by the time they reached their destination he would be close to exploding into action and wondered whether that might help or hinder his chances of success.

The land beyond the river was uniformly flat and close to featureless. Everywhere there were plain and exposed fields, the grass short and studded with thick clumps of reeds that fed eagerly on the wet soil. Carving this immense expanse of pasture into irregular-shaped fields were water-filled ditches and raised dykes that must have run for hundreds of miles in total. Sheep seemed to be the chief means by which farmers made a living and there were large numbers of these hardy animals to be seen stoically ignoring the wind as they grazed.

Away to their left, maybe five or six miles inland there was a short run of low-lying hills, beyond which, Templeman had seen on his map, lay villages such as Tenterden. Once upon a time the sea had reached that far inland and there had been a thriving boatbuilding industry along that stretch of coastline.

To their right, beyond the last of the fields, were low, irregular-shaped sand dunes that provided a little shelter from the vastness of the sea and somewhere out there, he was sure, even now lay at anchor a German yacht, waiting for a signal from the lighthouse.

After a while they passed close to the Rye links golf course, laid out amongst the sand dunes. Just visible on the far side of the course was the club's own halt on the little tram line that ran out of Rye and on along the coast to a tourist spot they would be reaching in a little while.

The carter said little as they travelled, which suited Templeman well. His mind was so tightly focused on the business ahead that he feared he would make a poor conversationalist. He, instead, began to consider how matters might play out once he reached the lighthouse, analysing them over and over again, a little tweak here, a new possibility there. All the while, his nerves were preying on him, feasting on his weaknesses and insecurities. He did at least have the reassurance of the cool metal of his gun whenever he slipped a hand into his pocket. It was his only assistance, though one he still didn't relish resorting to.

"There it is," said the carter, his voice twanging with the countryside, as they emerged from the shelter of a battered copse of trees showing the first signs of coming into leaf.

Templeman looked to their right, where, perhaps a mile away, he could clearly see the lighthouse. For a moment its imposing structure looking immense and powerful as a ray of sunlight swept over it. Then, as the sunlight moved away, the lighthouse took on a brooding, though still powerful presence and Templeman felt as if it was observing his approach, already aware of his mission. He wondered if it would be friend, foe or an uncommitted bystander who had seen many men die under its gaze on stormy, unforgiving days and nights when the sea claimed its helpless victims.

Was that to be him, another helpless victim, even if it was a German agent's gun rather than the sea that took his life? He shook his head. If that was to be the way of things, he'd see to it that he didn't make it easy for Von Luck's men. He'd make them risk everything in order to stop him, their own lives included.

Presently, they came to the small hamlet of Lydd, which seemed to consist entirely of modest two-storey timber and brick buildings. In a good many cases, their wooden facias were weather-beaten in the extreme, the paint flaking away in sheets and the windows so heavily salt-stained it was impossible to see through them. The sound of metal being beaten rang out as they passed a forge and they found the street busy with people going about their business as they reached the main thoroughfare.

Here the carter turned right, on to a narrow dirt track that ran away towards the sea. As they did so, Templeman pulled out his pocketwatch once more. Thirty-four minutes had now passed since they left the town.

"'Tis a bleak spot down here," commented the carter, sweeping his gaze across the scene before them. "All this land was left by terrible storms centuries back," he informed his passenger.

Templeman too surveyed the strip of land that lay between themselves and the sea. If the landscape had seemed harsh and exposed before, it was as nothing compared to what they now encountered. For one thing, the wind had picked up and was now gusting energetically into their faces, the sea salt it carried easy to taste when it blew across the lips.

Within a minute they left behind the last of the grassland and the small, beaten trees and entered into another world. A more isolated and inhospitable spot it was difficult to imagine. Everywhere there was shingle; great sheets of it running off in all directions, punctuated here and there by blobs of green that were some remarkable species of plant-life able to survive in such conditions, clinging to the ground like limpets. And the wind swept in off the sea in surging, powerful blasts that made their cart wobble more than usual.

The flatness of the scene was broken only by a few clusters of wooden fishermen's shacks huddled together for shelter, their timbers so heavily beaten they looked as if they might collapse at any moment. A few small boats had been dragged up on to the shingle and their rigging, where it remained, whipped and whined in the wind.

It was beyond these last few remnants of civilisation that Templeman could finally cast his gaze on the sea, which rolled and swelled in a manner that suggested evil intent. An endless succession of waves tumbled on to the beach, the sounds of their arrival lost amongst the roar of the wind.

Here and there a seagull loitered on the wind, calling sharply to its fellows, or sweeping down to inspect some piece of detritus being carried by the sea. How these birds were able to manage with such ease in this hostile environment, Templeman found quite remarkable.

The agent blinked into the wind as the cart cleared an especially rough stretch of ground. He looked across to their right, to where he could now clearly see the lighthouse. It was a huge, rounded sentinel, unmoving and unyielding against the worst that nature could throw at it. Standing a little inland from the sea, the main body of the lighthouse was joined at the base, on the landward side, by a small one-storey building. Lying on the shingle next to this was an upturned rowing boat.

The track to the lighthouse, such as it was, took a turn to the right as they closed in on the sea, bringing them some four hundred yards short of their destination. With so very little cover to hide their approach, it occurred to Templeman that he would easily enough be seen by any lookout at the lighthouse. That might very well result in his receiving the kind of hot welcome he could do without.

His options were few, but they had just reached one of those rare clusters of weather-beaten wooden shacks, the last they would pass before arriving at the lighthouse.

"That's close enough, thank you," he instructed the carter, having to raise his voice in order to overcome the relentless roar of the wind. "I'll walk the rest of the way from here."

The carter didn't question the instruction, nor so much as cast a quizzical look at his passenger, but pulled up his plodding horse alongside a particularly broken down hut.

"As you wish," he said. "Sally here will be pleased enough to save a little on the journey. She's not so happy on this loose ground, is you, girl?"

The horse made no response, but kept its head low, turned towards the land and away from the worst of the wind.

Having climbed down on to the shingle, which at once began to shift ceaselessly under his feet, Templeman watched the cart being wheeled around and then beginning to retrace its steps, before he turned his attention back to the matter at hand.

"Well, here you are," he said to himself. "What now?"

It had occurred to him that, if the lighthouse was to be the location from which the German agents made their escape, any signal to a waiting yacht would best be sent after dark. That too would offer his adversaries the greatest cover under which to land a small boat on the beach. But that darkness also offered him cover, under which he could approach the lighthouse and put an end to any escape attempt.

Such an approach to the situation stretched his patience, but he knew he faced at least two opponents and very likely three or even four. Those odds would be too great for him to risk in broad daylight. It wasn't that he minded so much risking his life, since that was expected of someone in his line of employment and was the right thing for any patriot to do, but he would prefer to do so with at least some realistic chance of success. No, on this occasion he would need to pay heed to the old adage, act in haste and repent at leisure; he would need to be patient.

There was one other matter that agitated him and that was not knowing whether the German agents had already arrived at the lighthouse. He thought it most likely they had, since remaining in Rye would only expose them to the danger of arrest following the events at the Tower. But there was no sign of them here. No transport left outside the building. No guard beside the entrance. Without entering the building he could not be certain either way.

And what of the lighthouse keeper? From what the carter had said, it seemed unlikely the man would be the sort to be bought. Perhaps the Germans simply planned to overpower him. But that too remained uncertain; another factor to complicate the situation.

Templeman looked again at his watch. There were, perhaps, two and a half hours until dusk. Another twenty minutes or so after that and it ought to be dark enough for him to approach the lighthouse unseen.

He turned to the ramshackle building he was standing beside, pulled away two of the least resistant timbers and squeezed inside. The place was gloomy, damp and reeked of the sea. It had probably done service as some sort of store room, but now there was nothing more than a few abandoned crates and bits and pieces of fisherman's equipment, none of which looked serviceable to his inexpert eye. He dragged one of the more sturdy crates across the floor to the wall on the far side and positioned it next to a gap in the timbers through which he could observe the lighthouse. Sitting on the crate, he pulled his coat more tightly about him, took a deep, resigned breath and began his vigil.

A BOLD STEP

Templeman came to with a start as his head slipped forward along the wooden wall and he fell off the crate on to the floor. He opened his eyes, confused, forgetting for a moment where he was, then cursed himself for being so careless as to fall asleep.

Dragging himself back up on to the crate, he yawned, stretched out his arms, then peered outside. It was now all but dark, the last vestiges of light lingering over the landscape. The wind whipped and swirled as before, rattling some of the looser timbers in the hut, and in all respects the scene he took in was unchanged from how it had looked before fatigue took over.

Had Von Luck's men arrived while he was sleeping? Were they now ensconced in the lighthouse, ready to make their signal to the waiting yacht? He chided himself again, annoyed that he had made matters all the more uncertain through his own carelessness. The time had come, perhaps, for him to make his way to the lighthouse. There was a little remaining cover and, as for the rest of the open and exposed ground, he would just have to trust to luck and the growing darkness.

But as he rose to squeeze his way back out of the hut, his ears picked up a new sound. It was difficult to make out at first, coming and going as the wind gusted. As he stood there listening, the sound became more persistent and louder, until he could clearly make out that it came from some sort of engine.

He stepped across to the wall facing towards the sea and found a narrow gap through which he could see the approach to the lighthouse. Not more than seventy yards away was an open-top motor vehicle, making its way along the track, its wheels struggling for purchase in the shingle.

As it passed the hut, he could see there were four men in the vehicle. One of these, he could make out, was carrying what appeared to be a significant injury and sitting in the back next to him was the tall man Templeman recognised from the Ypres Tower. If this confirmation that the Germans were not yet safely secured in the lighthouse was welcome news, what was most certainly unwelcome was seeing that he would be facing four adversaries.

Templeman rubbed a hand across his chin and his brow narrowed. The challenge ahead of him was going to be a major one indeed with the odds being so heavily in favour of the Germans. He pulled his gun from his pocket and checked to see how many bullets remained. There were four, one for each enemy agent. He grimaced. His shooting, if it came to that, was going to need to be very accurate indeed.

When the vehicle came to a stop outside the lighthouse, the two men in the front stepped down on to the gravel and moved furtively towards the small outhouse, disappearing inside for a brief while. When they re-appeared, they moved with care up to the entrance of the lighthouse itself and, in a manner that made it clear they were not invited guests, crept inside.

Now, Templeman told himself. Now was his time to act. If, as appeared to be the case, the first two men were setting about securing the lighthouse for their purposes while the taller man remained with their injured colleague, then, for now at least, the odds were but two to one. This was his moment. The enemy had helpfully split its forces, throwing away the best of their advantage.

Templeman emerged from the same gap as he'd entered, keeping the building between him and the two remaining Germans. However, as he rounded the corner intending to make for the cover of the sole shack that remained between him and the lighthouse, he saw the taller enemy agent helping his colleague off the vehicle and into the outhouse. Once again they had inadvertently done him a favour, since it now looked likely he would be able to cover the open ground with little risk of being seen.

Waiting for the two men to disappear inside the building, he then made his way as quickly as he could over the shifting shingle, his feet struggling for purchase, so as to approach the outbuilding on the windowless landward side. By the time he reached the building, pressing himself up against the wall so as to minimise his profile, his heart was racing and his breathing had become shallow and rapid.

He pulled the gun from his coat pocket, then nearly lost his grip on it, so sweaty were the palms of his hands. Opening the cylinder once more, he counted the bullets again then snapped it shut. He took two long, deep breaths, then moved along the side of the wall. Pausing at the corner to make sure neither of the enemy agents who had gone into the lighthouse had re-appeared, he pushed on to the entrance of the outbuilding.

A single drop of sweat ran down the side of his face from the temple and he wiped it away before he pressed an ear to the door. Sounds came from the inside. Voices and someone moving around, it seemed, but it was all too indistinct for him to make out clearly. That did at least suggest the two men inside were some distance from the doorway and Templeman wondered if there might be some sort of entrance hall for him to clear first, or if it was just a single, open space inside.

He reached nervously for the worn and pitted wooden door handle then pulled himself up short, realising, with alarm, that he hadn't considered what he was actually going to do once he was inside. Ought he simply to shoot the two men and, if so, could he bring himself to gun them down in cold blood like that? Or perhaps he should look to disarm them and lock them in the building, perhaps tie them up, if rope could be found. The latter held far more appeal. Yes, that's what he would aim for.

The handle turned easily and the door gave freely as he began to ease it ajar. Every instinct he possessed was screaming at him not to go on and it took more inner strength than he would have thought he possessed to keep pushing it steadily open, his gun held out in front of chest.

When the opening reached the point where he could squeeze through and still no challenge had come from within, Templeman slipped inside the building, pushing the door to behind him. He found himself in a narrow entrance hall that was packed with a myriad of detritus and reeked of damp. Voices came through the open doorway ahead of him that seemed to lead into some larger storage room.

Now so tense that he could hardly move, Templeman moved across the entrance hall and peered cautiously into the room beyond. There, over by the far wall, the taller German agent had sat his injured colleague in what appeared to be the only chair in the room and was now searching through some cupboards.

Templeman battled in vain to slow the thumping in his chest, then, sliding his forefinger on to the trigger, he brought the gun to bear on the taller German and stepped into the room.

"I would prefer it if you'd stop right where you are," he said, surprised at his choice of words, which struggled to escape his dry mouth.

The tall man froze, bent over one of the cupboards. The injured German agent seemed not to have even noticed Templeman's arrival.

"Hands above your head," he instructed the taller man.

The German began to lift his left hand up as instructed but before it quite reached his head, he swung round, bringing his right hand up as he did so. The gun he was holding flashed once and, before Templeman had time to fully realise what was happening, a bullet crashed into the wall beside his head.

The Englishman squeezed the trigger on his own weapon and was rewarded by the sight of the enemy agent falling back against the cupboard, letting out a shout of pain as he did so. Templeman had aimed for the man's stomach and it seemed he had scored a direct hit.

But in the moments Templeman spent taking this in, the German got away a second shot and this one was better aimed, the bullet cutting through the outside of Templeman's left arm, a little above the elbow. He winced at the burning pain and cursed his ineptitude as he dropped down behind the partial cover of a workbench to his left.

The German pulled his left hand away from his stomach and even from the other side of the room Templeman could see it was covered with blood.

"You're wounded," he called out to the German agent. "There's no point in you trying to go on. You'll simply be throwing away your life. Come on now, toss your gun on the floor and put your hands up."

The answer to Templeman's challenge came without delay, a flurry of bullets thudding into the wall above his head as the German pulled himself upright, apparently intent on rushing the Englishman's position. Taking aim through the space under the top of the workbench, Templeman fired two more shots. They both found their mark and the man from the Bureau watched with relief as the gun slipped from the German's fingers and he collapsed to the floor.

Templeman let out a sigh of relief and allowed his chin to rest for a moment on his chest. He was still alive and that had not been something he had taken for granted as he'd entered the building. Another deep breath and then he rose to his feet.

The second German had not moved a muscle during the brief gun fight and, as Templeman looked down on him, he could see the man was unlikely to survive much longer. His face was white, his eyes closed and his breathing so shallow as to be almost non-existent. He was no threat.

Having then confirmed the other German was indeed dead, Templeman searched the man's pockets and quickly found what he was looking for, a small supply of bullets. He knew that his own gun was now almost out of ammunition, so set it to one side and, with hands that he realised were now no longer quivering, the man from the Bureau picked up the German's discarded weapon, loaded it, then snapped it shut. The first part of his improvised plan had been a total success. Now for what would most likely prove to be the more difficult part, dealing with the two Germans in the lighthouse.

He was on the point of leaving the room when Templeman stopped, all of a sudden aware that there was something he had neglected to do. The key to Meyer-Hoffman's security box. He returned to the two Germans, starting with the dead man, and searched through their pockets. Neither had the key on them. A shame, thought the Englishman. If he had found the key there, he would have been in a position to return to Rye without the need to take on the other two German agents.

The heat of battle seemed to have brought to life all his natural instincts for survival and he felt a sharpness and awareness of everything around him that he could not recall having experienced before. It was as if he had become another person altogether. That could only be a good thing. Had he remained the bag of nerves he'd been up until then, he doubted his chances of success would have been high.

He stepped out of the small building, looked up at the lighthouse with a cool, calm detachment, then made for the entrance, his approach steady and resolute.

TO RISK IT ALL

A small light mounted high on the wall above him let off a faint glow, picking out the first few steps on the stairs that faced Templeman as he closed the heavy door behind him. The hinges let out a soft, well-practised complaint, then fell silent. The Englishman stood motionless, his ears searching for sounds of movement from above.

At first he heard nothing more than faint traces of the wind that continued to sweep in from the Channel. But as he was about to set foot on the first thick stone step, the echo of a voice reached down to him. He stood still and listened. The same voice came again, then a second one, louder than the first. Men were shouting and at least one of them, he could just make out, was doing so in German. Then the raised voices became mingled, two or more men speaking at the same time, before being cut through with a loud, echoing explosion, then another. Someone was firing a gun.

Then all was quiet again. Templeman waited to see what might unfold, suspecting it could only mean one thing. The lighthouse keeper had objected to the intrusion of his two unexpected guests and this had descended into an argument, brought to an end by one of the Germans. He felt a ripple of disgust. The shooting of an unarmed man was an evil perpetrated by only the very worst of human beings.

Having waited a little longer and there still being no further signs of activity from above, Templeman concluded that the Germans must have resumed their climb towards the top of the lighthouse. After all, that was the best place from which to make a signal. But whether or not he was right didn't much matter; he needed to press on. He began to edge his way up the first flight of spiral steps, keeping close to the inside wall, his gun held up in front of his chest. His injured arm throbbed and burned, but he pushed aside the pain and focused on the task at hand, determined that nothing would get in his way.

As he closed on what he could now see was the first of the upper floors, the space became ever more brightly lit by the flickering of a gas light, casting a warm glow on the hard, cold stonework around him. Presently, he came to a length of wooden balustrade that sectioned off the stairwell from the room beyond. He paused to listen once more and, hearing no sound of any sort, crept on until he could lean forward and peer through the first of the gaps in the balustrade.

He found himself at floor level, looking into a single room. It seemed, from the presence of a pair of heavily worn armchairs and a short, wide bookcase packed with a medley of volumes, that he had reached some sort of sitting room. There being no sign of the two Germans, he pushed on up the remaining stairs and stepped into the room.

Flames flickered and crackled in a fireplace built into the far wall and a row of framed photographs sat on a narrow shelf above this. But Templeman's gaze was then arrested by the sight of a man's body, sprawled on the floor in front of the fireplace. Bearded and bald, most likely beyond his fiftieth birthday, he lay on his back, open, unblinking eyes staring up at the ceiling. His thick woollen jumper was stained red and a pool of blood had spread across the floorboards.

Templeman checked, unsuccessfully, for a pulse, closed

the man's eyes, then stepped away and leaned against the wall, feeling nauseous. It took a moment to regain control of his senses. What needless, violent slaughter. Surely they could simply have tied the man up? He ground his teeth together silently and felt a growing anger well up inside him.

But thoughts of revenge were broken by another burst of sound, as voices echoed down the stone steps that led upwards through an open doorway to his left. He stepped closer and listened again. Men were talking, of what he could not make out, for the voices seemed far away. He could see light flickering through another open doorway at the top of this run of steps but had the clear impression the voices were not in that room.

Casting aside some caution as anger began to take hold of him, Templeman cleared the steps in half the time he had taken on the first set and found himself looking into a small kitchen. It was, in every respect, an exemplary example of tidiness and order, not a thing out of place, although the smell of cooked fish hung heavy in the air.

As he surveyed the room, a thought came to Templeman. Pulling open a narrow wooden drawer he at once found what he was looking for: a kitchen knife, its sharp, pointed six-inch blade glinting in the gas light. Pulling up a trouser leg, he slipped the blade of the knife inside his sock and dropped the trouser leg back in place. He may well have six bullets in his gun, but he faced the prospect of taking on two enemy agents and it might well come down to hand-to-hand fighting; better he be prepared for such an eventuality.

The voices from above had ceased, which unnerved the Englishman somewhat. There was a security, of sorts, in hearing the other men talk, since it allowed him to know where they were. Now he would have to continue his advance with renewed caution, or risk running straight into Von Luck's men.

Another flickering light at the top of a further run of steps led him into a large storage room. As well organised as the kitchen, here were neat rows of crates, large and small, on two sides of the room. He lifted the corner of the lid on one crate to find it contained a tin of paraffin, the strong smell of which crept into his nostrils.

On the far side of the room was another set of stairs but these ones were wooden; thick sections of greyed oak with well-worn grooves in the centre of each tread. Templeman hesitated at the first step, conscious that, whereas stone steps made no sound, wooden ones had a habit of creaking and squeaking as you navigated them.

He stared up into the dimly-lit space above him. It appeared the stairs took a dog-leg turn, coming back on themselves, and he surmised there would be no more rooms to work through before he reached the top of the lighthouse, where he would find the housing for the light itself. That, surely, had to be the place from which the German agents would make their signal to the waiting yacht?

With great caution, Templeman placed a foot on the first of the wooden steps and leaned into it. The length of timber took his weight without complaint. He took another step, then another and by the time he had reached the landing where the stairs switched back, he felt more confident they would not betray him.

It was as he reached the landing that he again heard voices from above, but this time they were much closer and he could easily make out the two individuals involved. He wished his German was better, so that he might have an idea of what they were saying, but it made no real difference to his intentions and he took hold of the next stretch of banister, keen to bring matters to a head.

But the banister shifted to one side, the joint having come loose, and the Englishman stumbled. He froze, holding his breath and listening intently. There was no pause in the conversation from above and Templeman let out a gentle sigh, thankful his approach appeared to remain undetected. The numbers were in his enemies' favour but he felt confident the confrontation would be an evenly matched one if only he could hold on to the advantage of surprise.

Reaching the end of the second flight of wooden stairs, Templeman found a very different prospect now lay ahead of him. The next flight opened out into a broad space with a high ceiling. The voices of the two Germans, talking intermittently now, echoed down the stairs. One of them seemed to be issuing commands to the other. Light filled this open space and yet something seemed amiss.

It took a moment for Templeman to realise what wasn't right. They were at the top of the lighthouse now and the room he was staring up into housed the light itself. Given it was already dark, the light ought to be firing out its warning to passing ships, in which case the whole space should be so overwhelmingly bright that he would not be able to look into it. But he could. Although the space was well lit, the light was coming from nothing more than a series of gas lamps. Von Luck's men had wasted no time in going about their business by switching off the beam.

Steeling himself for what lay ahead, Templeman ran his tongue over his dry lips then pulled back the hammer on his revolver. This was it. The final confrontation. He thought again of the dying figure of Meyer-Hoffman, his widowed wife and the murdered lighthouse keeper and any lingering sense of fear or notions of flight were promptly set aside. This was for King and country, yes, but it was also for two ruthless, needless murders. Templeman began to creep up the final flight of stairs.

As he reached the top, he dropped on to his haunches so that he could look through the balustrade while staying at least partially concealed. Directly in front of him was a large open space, while to his left a short flight of steps led up to a platform which wrapped around three sides of the huge light's dome.

In the wooden wall underneath the dome there was a double-door that provided access to the workings of the light. He knew this because he could see a short, stocky man with dark brown hair sitting in front of the open doors fiddling with some wiring. The man had his back to

Templeman who could see the German agent's revolver laying on the ground a few yards away from where he sat. A voice called down from the upper deck and the shadow of a man moved across the floor, then disappeared.

It felt to Templeman as if every muscle in his body had grown tense and his senses were more alert by far than ever they usually were. There were some ropes hanging in coils from hooks on the wall at the back of the room and they helped to form a plan in the Englishman's mind. He would subdue the German in front of him, bind him, then move quickly on to face the one on the upper deck. If he could maintain the element of surprise he was confident of his chances. If he couldn't? Well, that was best not contemplated.

Setting himself for a quick movement, Templeman launched himself up and forwards, his gun aimed squarely at the enemy agent. But he had taken no more than a single step when his left foot hit some unseen object. A small tin of oil clattered across the floor.

Templeman hesitated, confused by the unexpected distraction, and glanced down at the can of oil. As he did so, the German looked round then threw himself across the floor, reaching for his gun. The Englishman, his heart thumping, took aim and fired off two shots. The German yelled out and fell to the floor. But, rather than lying there unmoving, he rolled over, now holding his gun, and fired a single shot. It crashed harmlessly into the wall high above Templeman's head. Templeman went to fire again then stopped. The German's weapon slipped from his grasp and his head fell back against the floorboards with a dull thud.

A shouted challenge broke the sudden silence and Templeman turned to see the second German agent stepping from behind the dome, his gun sweeping up in front of him. Before the Englishman could move, the German let off a shot and the bullet buried itself in a shower of splinters into the balustrade next to Templeman's left hip.

The English agent fired once at the German, then

launched himself across the room towards the cover of the short wooden wall where the dead man lay. Another bullet exploded from the German's gun and, passing over the diving target, ricocheted off the far wall with a sharp ping as flakes of stone flew through the air.

Templeman dragged himself up into a crouched position, breathing heavily, his ribs sore from the violent impact with the floor. Peering towards the steps to the upper deck, the man from the Bureau wondered how either of them would now be able to move in for the kill without exposing themselves entirely.

But the German agent must have come to the same conclusion, for there was no immediate sign of him. Was he considering his options? Perhaps he was still attempting to signal his compatriots out at sea. Might they send reinforcements? That was not a happy thought. No, decided Templeman, he could not afford to remain where he was for long. Somehow or other, he had to take back the initiative.

Then all at once the world around him exploded in a hail of bullets, thudding into the timbers of the wooden wall and floorboards. The bullets were coming from his right. The German had made his way to the far end of the platform, on the other side of the dome, and was firing over the edge at Templeman's position.

Firing almost blind in the direction the German, Templeman hurled himself towards the steps to the upper deck. A bullet crashed against his gun, ripping it from his grasp and sending it flying across the room. The pain in his hand was intense and, as he rolled on to the stairs and out of sight of the German, Templeman paused to find his fingers were coated with blood.

Footsteps hurried towards him and Templeman prepared himself for the worst. Injured and without a weapon, it seemed he was to fall short in his mission after all and an unexpected calmness began to fall over him. But as it did so, he remembered the knife he had picked up in the kitchen. Tugging up his trouser leg, he pulled it from its hiding place, its warm wooden handle feeling reassuring in his grasp.

"Templeman," snarled a Germanic voice from the top of the stairs. "You have done much damage, but I will put an end to it now."

The Englishman looked up to see a wide-eyed face glaring down at him. The man's right hand held his revolver in a tight grip and it was aimed directly at Templeman. Well, the odds were not good, but he'd rather go down fighting than allow the German to finish him off where he was, meekly and without resistance.

Hurling himself towards the German, Templeman swept the knife up in front of him, intent on driving it into his enemy as hard and deep as he could.

The German laughed and stepped swiftly to one side, tripping the Englishman so that he clattered to the floor, his knife slipping from his grasp.

"Do you think we are not trained for such fighting?" came the taunting challenge from the grinning German.

"You won't get far," replied Templeman, struggling to recover his breath. "The Royal Navy will chase you down before you leave the Channel."

"I think not," said the German, his grin now gone, replaced with a cold, calculating stare. "Goodbye, Templeman."

The German took aim at Templeman and, without a moment's hesitation, pulled the trigger. The metallic sound of the hammer striking the body of the gun was the only noise that echoed in the space between the two men. The German tried a second time, with the same result.

Seizing his opportunity, Templeman dashed to one side and snatched up his knife. As he did so, the German agent launched himself at the Englishman, swinging at him with his gun. They clashed, then fell away from each other, the man from the Bureau circling round so that his back was to the dome of the light, his opponent matching his moves.

Templeman jabbed out with his knife, but the German easily evaded the attack and, for a brief moment, the two men stood silent and motionless, each waiting for the other to move. Then, with a surprising swiftness that almost caught out the Englishman, the German lunged forward, peeling out to his right before coming back at Templeman, who stepped away, sweeping the knife round in front of him as he did so.

The German cried out and took a half step back, a hand reaching up to his face, blood running freely from a gapping wound in his left cheek. He snarled, reset himself, then launched another attack.

This time the English agent took only a half step to his left and brought the knife in hard and straight, ducking his head forward to escape the gun that swept towards him in a wide arc. He felt the blade of the knife sink into the soft flesh of the German's belly and, as he had been trained to do, he twisted the knife before pulling it out.

The German staggered and looked down at his belly. His face was filled with shock, already growing a little pale and his mouth open. He was right in front of the opening he had made in the outer glass housing, though Templeman thought later that he must not have realised that was so. Now, unsteady on his feet, the German stumbled and fell backwards, catching the edge of the opening. As he did so, his hands fell down at his sides, the gun clattering to the floor and, perhaps thinking he would prop himself up against the glass wall, went to lean back, only to fall through the opening. He fell silently into the darkness and was gone.

COUNTING THE COST

Alexander Templeman stood on the restless shingle that shifted continually under his feet and stared out towards the sea, a dark, inky current that sighed as it lapped around his shoes. Here and there, where gaps opened in the cloudy sky, stars would twinkle in the darkness before being washed away by the sweeping beam from the lighthouse that rose up behind him.

Police and medics had arrived some half an hour earlier and there had been a constant hubbub of voices and the crunching of shingle as they had set about their various tasks. Another motor vehicle rumbled its way across the shingle and pulled up alongside those already parked in a neat row in front of the lighthouse outbuilding.

Somewhere out in the watery darkness a ship sounded its horn, a long deep warning to others to be aware of its presence. From amongst the ramshackle buildings away to his left an agitated dog replied, its short, sharp barks feeble by comparison.

Templeman heard footsteps approaching from behind and broke himself away from his contemplation of the day's events to see Chief Inspector Mauldling of the Sussex Constabulary walking his way.

A nondescript fellow with old fashioned big, bushy whiskers, he had been rather excited on arrival, bringing with him, it seemed to Templeman, entire the entire force at his disposal. The place had quickly been swamped with uniformed officers, all looking for something to do. Many, roused from their beds in the early hours, had appeared to still be half asleep, wandering around uncertainly and silently with tired, half-closed eyes. The chill of the night had soon woken them, however, and the pace of their work had quickly picked up.

But Mauldling had been eager and alert from the start, issuing orders to one group of men then promptly turning to another to give them instructions. And, when he had been satisfied that all was in hand, he had turned his attentions to Templeman, assuring him he was in the know and there to help his mission, not hinder.

Mauldling had been summoned from his bed by Eastwood, whom Templeman had spoken to a short while before from the post office in Lydd. The Postmaster had not been at all pleased at finding the agent hammering on his door, demanding access to a telephone, but he had eventually come around once Templeman had told him he needed to make a call to the police.

Now it was close to eleven o'clock and the Chief Inspector had news to report.

"Hello there, Templeman. Hard to believe, sometimes, there's another country out there, just a few miles distant," he said, with a sharp, military snap to his voice, as he looked out to sea. "On a night as dark as this, France might as well be on the other side of the planet."

Templeman managed a thin smile. "Yes, I do believe you're right about that."

"Well, then, you'll no doubt be pleased to know our work here is almost done. I will, of course, have a man remain stationed here until your colleagues make it down from London. Don't want any uninvited visitors interfering with the scene."

"Very good of you. I feel rather guilty having not contacted you sooner, after the events at the Ypres Tower, but... well..."

"No need to apologise," cut in the Chief Inspector. "Where it's a matter of national security that's involved, you must do what needs to be done. I know there was no offence intended and there's certainly none taken."

An ambulance's engine rumbled into life behind them.

"Thank you for your understanding," said Templeman. "I know all this will very likely cause more than a few problems for you."

"Nothing that can't be addressed with a firm hand and a little imagination," replied Mauldling, pulling his thick woollen coat more tightly about him. "Damn wind cuts right through a chap's clothes out here. Don't know how the fellows who work on the coastline last more than a day."

"It is rather desolate," observed Templeman.

"That's the first two bodies being removed to Hastings Hospital," said Mauldling, nodding towards the ambulance that was now making its way along the all but invisible track towards Lydd and the main road. "We'll have the others loaded up and on their way shortly. I've had some of my men search the whole place from top to bottom to make sure we remove any weapons and other items that belonged to these Germans. Eastwood asked us to hold on to it back at the station. Mind you, it's hard to be certain which items were theirs."

Templeman fingered the little key he had stowed away in a coat pocket. He had found it on the body of the German agent who had fallen from the top of the lighthouse. Searching his pockets had not been a pleasant affair, but, having by then checked all the other Germans, Templeman had been left with no alternative. As soon as he had found the key, he had breathed a sigh of relief. Without it, things would have been very difficult for the Bureau. There were limits beyond which even it could not step and a complete search of every security deposit box in every bank in London would have been a step too far.

"I imagine my colleagues will be hoping there are some helpful items or pieces of intelligence to be found on the dead men," replied Templeman, not wanting to be too specific. "It's not the type of opportunity that comes along every day."

"I should rather hope not," remarked the Chief Inspector. "I have to say, it's quite an incredible job you've done here. Don't know how you managed it. Says a great deal for the sort of men you chaps are and the training they must put you through. Sets my mind quite at ease about the safety of the country."

"Quite honestly, Chief Inspector, I have no idea myself how it is I am standing here, alive and in one piece. I can only say that, as you observe, the excellent training plus a good slice of luck are responsible."

Templeman rubbed his arm where one of the many bullets fired at him had found its target. It was bandaged now, the bleeding stopped, but it still throbbed with pain. Yes, he thought to himself, he had indeed enjoyed more than his fair share of good fortune.

"Ah," said Mauldling. "Here comes Dr Eustace. Wonder what news he has for us?"

The doctor was an unusually tall man and as slim as a beanpole. He had to bend a little against the wind and held on to his small, round wire glasses with one hand all the while.

"Chief Inspector," he said, as he reached them. "Mr Templeman. Thought you should know my work here is all done and I will be returning home, unless there is anything else you have for me."

He spoke in a calm and precise manner that, to people who knew him more than a little, reflected well the man that he was.

"The injured fellow in the outbuilding, definitely a goner is he?" asked Mauldling, sounding rather disappointed.

"Yes, he is now dead. That stomach wound needed very

prompt treatment if he was to have any chance of surviving. The blood loss was considerable."

"Well, all for the best, I suppose," suggested the Chief Inspector, as a particularly strong blast of wind whipped around them.

Dr Eustace looked directly at Templeman. "I knew of Dr Meyer-Hoffman," he said. "Never had the pleasure of meeting the man, at least not while he was still alive, but I have a passing interest in the work being done to develop new gases for medical use. I've read some of his earlier work and it still leads the field. A sad loss to the medical profession."

"It is, indeed," replied Templeman. He did not want to stray into a discussion about Meyer-Hoffman's more recent work, nor why it was he had arrived in the country, so he turned to a more practical question. "Where has his body been removed to?"

"Hastings Hospital. It is the only one in the vicinity with the necessary capacity," replied Dr Eustace.

Templeman thought again of Meyer-Hoffman's wife and the terrible news she would be receiving all too soon. As he did so, he couldn't but think also how close his Caroline had come to finding herself a widow. He shuddered and batted the thought away. If he was to remain at the Bureau, such images could not be allowed to linger in his mind and he knew, for certain now, that he would continue as a secret service agent.

Though he might still have a good deal to learn, all those doubts that had plagued him about his competence for the job had gone. This mission had not been altogether a success, but it had shown him, beyond doubt, that he had what it took to do the job and the coming years were sure to bring plenty of opportunity for him to do so again.

The Sultan of Zanzire

A SIGN OF THINGS TO COME

The flint built church sat atop a small hill on the southern outskirts of the Kent village of Barnhurst. Its graveyard wrapped around three sides of the church and the little party of mourners was huddled together alongside a freshly cut grave on the western side. Here the land ran down towards a tiny, sparkling stream that had cut its way into the chalk over the course of many centuries. The vicar, a slim young man with sad eyes and a long, narrow nose, was reading from a small, worn Bible and two young children looked quizzically at the coffin, inside which lay their German uncle. A short woman dressed from head to foot in black sobbed quietly into a handkerchief, consoled by the embrace of a second woman.

Standing at the top of the slope, observing proceedings from afar, were four men dressed in mourning attire. One of them had an arm in a sling. All three watched intently and in silence. The widow, Mrs Meyer-Hoffman, had asked that her husband's funeral be solely a family affair, though had subsequently agreed to let the men from the Bureau attend on the understanding they would maintain their distance. The death of her husband had broken her entirely and she still held Sir Joshua in no small part responsible for what had

149

happened.

When, at last, the coffin had been lowered into the grave, the vicar had folded away his Bible and the small party of mourners turned away towards the church, the four men on the top of the slope relaxed a little and felt free to speak as they began the short walk back to their motor vehicle.

"I've heard this morning from Cambridge University," said Sir Joshua. "that Professor Whitehouse and Sir David Youngman will be picking up Meyer-Hoffman's work. I'm told they are the best we have and Sir David knew Meyer-Hoffman personally. Met the doctor on a couple of occasions. They'll be working closely with Anthony Marksman of McMaster and Gunnings, who are building a new manufacturing plant in Birmingham to turn out supplies of the new chemical weapons."

"Thank Heavens that Meyer-Hoffman had the presence of mind to lock his papers safely away in that security deposit box," added Vivian Eastwood. "Without those there wouldn't have been anything for us to work from and Lord knows how badly things might have turned out."

"Quite so," responded Sir Joshua. "It's been a heavy price for his widow to pay, it must be acknowledged, but his sacrifice will save a good many lives in the years ahead, of that I am sure."

Iain Moreland, walking with the aid of a stick, spoke next. "I hear a pair of German agents were arrested attempting to break into the Johnston-Appleton Laboratories at Cambridge University last night."

"They were," replied Eastwood. "Bit of a botched attempt, no doubt done in a hurry. Probably hoping to retrieve Meyer-Hoffman's papers, not that it would have done them much good now that we have made several copies."

"And what about Von Luck," asked Moreland, as the little group turned down the side of the church, following a narrow gravel path. "Has he paid the price for his failure in snatching back Meyer-Hoffman?"

"Our own agents in Germany seem to think he's escaped any serious consequences, although his stock appears to have dropped somewhat. I suppose his masters must have come to the conclusion that, with Meyer-Hoffman dead, we are in no position to benefit a good deal from his work. If so, they have badly misread the situation," answered Sir Joshua.

"Which would be all to our benefit," added Eastwood. "The less they know about our progress in developing these weapons, the better."

"That's very true," replied Sir Joshua, as they approached the road. "Now then, would you two continue on, please gentlemen," he added, turning to Moreland and Eastwood "I'd like to have a word with Templeman."

As the other two men walked ahead, Sir Joshua turned to Templeman.

"You've not said a word since we arrived," he observed.

"Can't help thinking I might have done more to keep Meyer-Hoffman alive," replied the younger man, somewhat reluctantly. "Seeing his widow here brought that thought back to me."

"It's unfortunate," replied Sir Joshua. "But these things happen to the best of us. We've all been where you are now, wondering if things might have turned out better if only we'd made a different choice or done something a little sooner. But hindsight is all well and good; at the time, we do what we believe needs to be done and in the manner we think best. In this case, given the odds you faced it's nothing short of a miracle and speaks volumes of your abilities that you managed to survive. You really mustn't go blaming yourself. You weren't the one who shot the doctor."

Templeman pursed his lips and nodded his head. "You're right, of course. I'm sure time will help me come to terms with things."

Sir Joshua glanced back in the direction of the main funeral party. "Mrs Meyer-Hoffman will be moving in with her sister and her family. They have a little estate on the outskirts of Shrewsbury. I'm sure she will get all the support and love she needs there. Best place for her."

"That's certainly good to hear," answered Templeman, genuinely relieved that the widow had someone to take care of her.

A huge black crow, sitting atop the church tower, barked out a message before taking to the wing and disappearing beyond a row of huge chestnut trees that lined the far side of the graveyard.

"Now then," said Sir Joshua, lowering his voice. "there's another matter I need to speak to you about. You ought to be aware that I've still not yet been able to unmask the traitor hiding in our midst. It seems that after, the events at Rye, they've decided they ought to lie low for a while. We've dangled two particularly tasty carrots under their nose this past week, but they failed to bite. Damned frustrating, but it seems we're going to have to remain patient and wait for them to recommence their activities."

"Yes, that's certainly is frustrating," replied Templeman. "Very frustrating indeed."

"Well, I suppose we can console ourselves that they won't remain inactive forever. No point in Von Luck having a man on the inside of the Bureau if he doesn't make any use of him and we'll be ready when he does start up his activities again."

They came to the church gate, with its angled wooden roof and the noticeboard showing the times of services, as well as an announcement of a forthcoming tea morning. The other two men were waiting for them and across the lane sat the motor vehicle in which Eastwood had driven them south.

"So, how are you feeling now?" asked Eastwood of Templeman. "That was quite some adventure you had in Rye."

"And in London," chided Moreland, smiling.

Eastwood laughed. "Of course. Mustn't forget that little flesh wound of yours."

"I have to say," began Templeman "that, apart from anything else, the whole affair has finally persuaded me that I do have what it takes to do this job. I felt a bit of a fraud before, nothing more than a chap who enjoyed an unusually good degree of luck. But now, after facing down Von Luck's men at the lighthouse, I finally believe I'm made of sterner stuff than I had thought before. Quite the lesson to learn, but I'm determined now to make the most of it."

"We never doubted you for one minute," replied Iain Moreland, leaning a little more heavily on his cane. "You can rest assured no one gets an invitation to join the Bureau unless we're as certain as we possibly can be that they have what it takes."

"Absolutely so," agreed Eastman, patting Templeman on the shoulder.

"You know," said Templeman. "I can't help recalling what Meyer-Hoffman said on the train up from Portsmouth, about civilisations resting on what are fundamentally weak foundations that can be undermined with terrifying ease. It seems to me that we might take a good deal too much for granted and really ought to be far more observant, ready to fend off those who would undermine this great civilisation of ours."

Iain Moreland paused as he was about to walk through the gate and when he spoke again there was a deeply serious tone to his voice. "Well, if it's war you're referring to, Templeman, then the likelihood seems to be coming closer every day. The situation in the Balkans is a powder keg just waiting for someone to set a light to it and that will happen soon enough. Then it's inevitable that all the Great Powers will become embroiled."

"And when that does happen," added Eastwood, "let us hope that it is a brief war."

"Hope," said Sir Joshua, pausing at the gate. "is a fine thing, but, sadly, not one that is always fulfilled. We might well choose to hope, and there's nothing wrong in that, but we should prepare for the worst. Now then, let's get back into your contraption, Eastwood, and commence our journey back to London. I've been dreading this as much as I did the trip down and I'd like to get it over and done with as soon as possible."

The four men climbed into the vehicle, now discussing the various merits and shortcomings of such new technology, and were soon driving down the narrow, hedge-lined lane away from the church and towards the London Road.

As they did so, a group of pigeons took to the wing in a hurry, spooked by some approaching danger. As one of them struggled to gain height, a sparrow hawk swept over a hedge, moving so quickly it was little more than a blur, and plucked the pigeon from out of the air. Moments later, the bird of prey, clutching the still living pigeon, came to rest in a grassy field where it began to gorge on its victim. It was a confrontation that was as sudden as it was short-lived and, on this occasion, the aggressor had come out on top.

Templeman turned away from the spectacle he had just witnessed and wondered to himself if it might hold some portent for what lay ahead for much of the world.

The End

If you enjoyed meeting Alexander Templeman then why not join him on his very first official mission as an agent of the British secret service. Sent to Vienna on a routine assignment to collect some important documents things quickly begin to go wrong and Templeman soon finds himself fighting for his life.

Download your free copy of *The Man from the Caucasus* now and prepare yourself to join Templeman as he battles for his life in a city he barely knows and facing a frightening adversary with all the cards stacked in his favour.

You can find out more about Ben Westerham at

www.benwesterham.com

and on various social media platforms.

From the David Good private investigator series

From 'Good Investigations'

"Mr Good," she purred like a hungry cat meeting a blind mouse, "and I do hope you will be." She slid beautifully, effortlessly in to the knackered old punter's chair, and I swear the thing wrapped itself lovingly around her sexy, lithe frame. Then she tempted me with those dark bewitching eyes, calling me closer, closer, closer

From 'Good Girl Gone Bad'

If you ask me, good girls can be the baddest there are, if the fancy takes them. Maybe it's because they save it all up for one big splurge, then go mad bad. I don't know, but what I do know is that anyone who tries telling you some little darling of theirs' wouldn't say boo to a goose is either stupid, misinformed or both. Any goody two shoes type should carry a health warning, 'Danger, Good Girl. May go bad at any moment'.

From the Banbury Cross Murder Mystery series

From 'The Hide and Seek Murders'

Eleanor Golightly never saw so much as a glimpse of the figure that moved up behind her, swift and silent, from the cover of the shrubbery. Indeed, she was only very briefly aware of the immense blow that came crashing down on her head. Just for a second or two, the world seemed to stop in silence, a peculiar sensation that she couldn't quite get to grips with before it had passed and she collapsed on to the immaculately cut lawn.

* * *